UNLEASHED

Joshua James Jordan

First paperback edition 2024

ISBN 9798334008731

www.JoshuaJamesJordan.com

CHAPTER 1: MAGILECTRIC

I've nearly died so often that nobody cares anymore. The first time, everyone dropped off a bunch of flowers. This go around, the hospital room's empty except for a card from Aunt Gracie that says: "Stop being dumb." My hospital bedsheets itch my skin, and it smells like they've been recycling the air here since the Industrial Revolution.

Only Emma's here because visiting a cousin is obligatory, right? She sits at the side of my hospital bed with her face saturated in pity. "Jake, you look terrible."

"You should see the other guy."

"I did. Marcus is fine."

"Whatever."

Opening the window and letting some real air in here would be nice. The room sits near the hospital's top, and the city's skyline stretches to the horizon. Dozens of cranes hover over the buildings like extinct giraffes grazing trees. The construction boom in Tallahassee started when I was in middle school, and it doesn't look like it has plans to stop.

"I'll beat him next time." The words come out almost as if I believe them. The benefit of being dumb is that lying to yourself is easy.

"Please don't. That was the last time. I don't want to visit you in here again." Emma fluffs the mop of hair on my head. She's the best replacement mom a guy could ask for.

"Nah. I'm a lot stronger than before. I'll keep practicing."

"Practicing, how? You don't even work at the plant to get familiar with what it's like not wearing your collar," Emma says. I almost forgot about it. I run the tips of my fingers along the cold metal that circles my neck.

The collars sense magical energy and then convert it into electricity. It's the same technology in the power plants, except the electricity shocks us instead so that we don't use our magic when we're not 'allowed.' They don't want us to use our power, though they have no problem using theirs against us. Their power being money.

"I practice through mental repetitions. I imagine myself fighting. It works. I read about it."

Emma rolls her eyes. "We're going to be scraping you off the field. By you, I mean your gooey remains and maybe some singed hair. I could put it in a locket and give it to your mother to remember you by."

"Yeah. Mom would appreciate that. She can trade it for some cigarettes. I'm glad you're here looking out for me, cuz."

Marcus strides into the room. He has dark skin, a black puff of hair, and a lean but still muscular frame, his biceps molded from clay. He's a little bit more fit than I am—just a little.

"Oh, God! Why are you here?" I sit up fast; a lightning bolt of pain races through my back, and my face contorts. I lean back down into the hospital bed slowly.

"Emma asked me to come," Marcus says in his deep voice.

"You did?" I ask Emma, lowering my voice an octave, too.

"Of course, I thought you guys were friends."

"No way, we're huge rivals."

"Nah. To be rivals, you both have to win sometimes," Marcus says. He crosses his arms and leans against the door frame.

"Look at his face," I say. "It always looks just like that. He could watch someone drop a bag of kittens into the ocean and still make that face."

"Why would you drown a bunch of kittens, Jake?" Emma asks.

"Not me. Like someone else. Ugh, just kill me already."

"We're here on our lunch break. You hungry? I could probably order something and deliver it by drone." Emma lifts her phone out of a small purse.

"Nope, because—"an IV bag stand towers over my bed, its wire winding down into my arm. I wrap the line around my hand twice and yank the IV out. "—we're all going back to school." I look down at the arm as the pain alarms ring in my head. "That's going to bleed a lot, isn't it? Hand me that washcloth, will you?"

Emma rolls her eyes and marches into the bathroom retrieving a first-aid kit instead. "You aren't going anywhere." She starts patching me up.

"I signed up for the evaluation today. No way am I going to miss it. Besides, I'm fine." I stand up. The world spins around. I close my eyes and take a deep breath, and it slows down. "See. I'm good." I head toward the hallway before Emma has even finished, tiny drops of my blood trail behind me.

My hospital gown remains open in the back, and cold air swishes over my butt. "Minty fresh," I say before passing my RoboDoc. It looks like a trash can with glowing green eyes and arms made of plastic tubes.

"Patient. Please return to your room," it says. An older model. It doesn't look like the newer androids equipped with magilectric batteries that can fly around and throw energy blasts.

"Gotta go, but as usual, your bedside manner was impeccable. Five out of five stars. Would almost die again. See ya!"

Emma bought her car with money from working at the plant. The cute little sedan shimmered in a color somewhere between red and pink. She's the only person I know who named her vehicle. She had named her car Rose, but I call it The Strawberry Wagon.

"Shotgun!" I limp towards the front door. Marcus gets in the back without contesting my claim.

Tallahassee has built so many new skyscrapers since the magilectric walls that hold back the ocean in Miami failed. Many people moved here from South Florida, afraid their whole city would soon be underwater. It's hard to imagine living in a place surrounded by towering walls of water. I wouldn't want to live there. I'm okay with just the one wall a dozen miles south.

The traffic picks up closer to noon as the businesses and government offices close for lunch. "We're going to be late," Emma says.

"Who cares?" I ask.

"I do," Marcus says.

"Yeah, some of us will actually graduate," Emma says.

"Shut up. I'm doing fine." Last time I checked, Ds are passing grades.

We turn a corner to approach our high school with little time to spare. The old brick building sits next to a newer, taller one with all glass exteriors. Seniors go to class in the old building and at the very top of the new building. Sophomores, like us, are stuck near the bottom where the best view held all the glamor of a parking garage and a dead tree.

"Hey Jake, you're going to have to get in the trunk," Emma says.

"Why? I'm legitimately coming back to school now."

"The security seems a bit buggy, and I just don't want to go through the hassle of it." She pulls over to the side of the road. "Go on."

The principal, one of the few actual human staff at the school, only allows students that work at the power plant to leave for lunch. He says it's a privilege only for those who give back to the world. Nothing's more fitting than coming back to school while trapped in someone's trunk like a coffin for a deadbeat like me.

I check my phone since there isn't much of a view from in there. "Tensions with Mars Reach Zenith!" Impeccable word choice. Zenith? They trying to do an astronomy pun? I never keep up with all the political stuff. I've got enough problems. I flip over to manage my fantasy football league because, hey, I can't be die losing at that.

Emma parks the car in the garage underneath the school. I hop out and two cute girls stand nearby, having just witnessed me hop out of the trunk like an animated bag of groceries.

"Good day, madams," I say in my best 17th-century gentlemen accent and bow. A breeze chills my butt as I bent down, and my gown parted in the back. The girls shake their heads and walk away.

"Such a ladies' man," Emma says.

"I'm an acquired taste."

"How long does it take to acquire this taste?"

"How long have we known each other?"

"All our lives."

"Longer than that then."

Marcus bounds off ahead of us, eager to see the matchups listed for today. I'm limping still, a sharp pain runs up my leg if I put too much pressure on it, so don't bother trying to keep up. Emma and I march up the garage stairs and enter one of the 10th grade floors. As we walk down a hallway, the collar on my neck vibrates, letting me know that class starts in a couple of minutes.

"Where're you headed?" I ask Emma. We pick which classes to attend. As long as there's a chair, you can go. Other schools have assigned schedules or watch lectures online. I prefer our way, not that I'm a big fan of schools at all.

"Magic energy," she says.

"That gets so boring after all these years."

"It's not boring if you aren't a weirdo and work at the plant. You realize how important it is to make energy, right?"

"You know why I don't work at the plant."

Emma smiles. "Aunt Jenna doesn't need to know that you work there. You have to take care of yourself."

"Yeah, I guess." She's not going to change my mind right now. No way am I going another boring energy class.

Cracks streak through the school's walls like lightning bolts. The deluge of new students has put a strain on the budget. The principal pretends malfunctioning teachers and ceiling water stains are normal. The whole building smells like an old wet book despite being built in the past ten years.

Other guys give Emma the double take as we head down the hallway. Girls never look at me that way. Or at all. After ogling her, one notices that I'm in a hospital gown.

"Nice dress," he says.

"Don't insult my culture."

We round a corner and Marcus some other students stands in front of a monitor in the hallway. Marcus towers over the rest and gives a wave.

"Hey, Jake. They posted our match-ups. I'm taking on a 1,000."

Marcus easily beat a droid with an 800 power rating a month earlier so he'd be able to take the next one. He grabbed the arm off the floor, walked over to the military officer, and asked, "This belong to you?" I went up against a 400 and just barely beat it. That was just a week ago.

"You've got that, no problem." All the heads bobbing around obscure the screen so I can barely see it. Usually, there'd be at least a dozen of us tested, but this time there's only three blurry names on the screen. Live feeds from the soccer field fill most of the screen. Other students can watch on these monitors or live online unless they cut the broadcast, which I've only seen once before.

"Guess what you got?" Marcus asks. I was almost close enough to see for myself. "400."

Relief washes through me. It's never good when they match you up with the same rating but, given how close it was last time, I just want to survive my battles. "That's too bad. I can handle more than that."

Marcus grins and holds up two fingers. "Not one. Two of them."

Someone laughs behind me and says, "You are so dead."

CHAPTER 2: THE SOUND OF SHRAPNEL

My collar buzzes with the two-minute warning. Gotta hurry. Nobody wants to be late for class. Trust me. We can all contemplate my imminent demise later. The crowd standing by the bulletin monitor disperses, losing interest as most had basically seen me die already. Emma's brow furrows, but I wave her off. "I'll see you after school. No way am I going to magilectric class."

Luis Gonzalez walks by from the opposite direction. He's the brightest guy I know, so attending class with him is always a good idea. Luis has long black hair in a ponytail and a slender frame. His goatee is thin, like he drew it on with a small marker. He's always got a tie on, even though our school doesn't have a dress code.

"Luis, what class are you going to?" I ask.

"History," he says. This dude's a mad scientist, kid-genius level smart. I wouldn't be surprised if he has a secret laboratory under his house. He's won engineering awards but doesn't bother attending math or science classes. He knows it all already.

"Me too, now."

After we get into the classroom, Luis sits down in the front, and I'd prefer to sit in the back with the others, but he always insists that you learn better up here. I hate it. You can't say a word; otherwise, the teacher would short-circuit.

The teacher's metal closet stands at the front of the room. This room's not on the edge of the building, but the wall monitors play a video feed from a park that makes it feel like we're in a larger space. The screen currently plays a loop of a guy tossing a Frisbee with his dog.

Our collars buzz: time to be in class. If you aren't in class on time...

"Ah!" A freshman flings open the door, leaps into the room, and sprawls out on the ground.

He rises to his knees, picks up his stuff, stands up, and then rubs his neck from the shock of the collar. "I'm never going to be late again. What class is this anyway?"

"History."

"Well, I guess I'm learning that today." He sits down in the back row.

The door opens again, and a girl I've never seen before strolls in. She doesn't scream or yell in pain at all. Strange. Her collar must be broken. She sits in the front row with Luis and me. She has long red hair and a powerful jawline that you'd see on a superhero. Muscular. She's like Super Ginger. Is that bad to say? Oh well.

What's even weirder than her not getting shocked is that she has a metal left arm and left leg. I've seen artificial limbs before, but never so close and never for this lon—

"What are you looking at?" she asks.

"Nothing," I say.

"Is my arm nothing?"

"Well, I don't know. I guess your arm is nothing now, and it's been replaced."

"Smooth," Luis says. "You'll have to pardon my friend. He just escaped the insane asylum."

"Ah, that explains the dress," she says. I really need to change my clothes.

The teacher comes to my rescue. The metal closet doors burst open, and a robot frame waltzes out. It jerks before the three projectors around the room flicker on, their beams spreading over the figure. A woman wearing a grey business suit with her hair up in a bun forms around the robot's frame. Like all our teachers, she must have been famous in her field at some point. They uploaded their personalities and voices into the teaching software and gave lectures to high school kids nationwide. The best teachers everywhere. Kind of.

The lecture begins, but I can't concentrate. I'm about to die, after all. Besides, the whole thing doesn't make sense. Why would they assign two bots with a 400 power rating when I had barely survived one a week ago? Did they want me to die? Almost nobody died from scrimmaging with bots after school. You were supposed to win. They just tested magical aptitude. They'd get so much bad press if one of the students died that they might have to cancel the program entirely.

The lecturer walks along the side of the class closer to the back to try and get the students' attention. The three of us in the front spun around.

"How'd you deactivate your collar?" I ask the new girl.

"I didn't," she says.

"Oh, come on. I can keep your secret."

"It works. Trust me."

I rolled my eyes. I wouldn't turn her into the principal, but I guaranteed somebody else would. If she isn't careful, she'll get into big trouble.

"What's your name?"

"Val."

"Like Valerie for short?" I ask. Dumb question, idiot, but my mouth is running ahead of my brain, just trying to converse with this girl.

"Yeah," she says.

"You!" The teacher bot points at me and starts walking over. "What did I say?"

"You said, uh, that the, uh—"

The metallic instructor slams her hand on the table in front of me, and the clang of her hand rings in my ear. "Let me paint this picture for you again. The ice caps were melting, the oceans encroached upon the world's most densely populated areas, mass evacuations, and the last reserves of carbon-based energy sources were depleted after decades of exploitation. Then what happens?"

"Um, magic?"

"That's right. The world's youth, that's you," she pokes my nose. The skin of her finger is just light, goes right through me, until the metal from the robot frame makes contact, "receive this gift of supernatural energy just when humanity needs it the most. We quickly harness its power, make walls to hold back the ocean, and save civilization as we know it."

Nobody can explain *why* this happened, though. A new force of the universe appears. Science is clueless, so we call it magic because we don't understand it. It must be rooted in *something* smart people like Luis can figure out.

"Seems like such a waste, though, to use up our power to hold back oceans."

"Ah," the teacher smiles, "but if the oceans cover more land mass, we lose arable land, and people would starve. You can see why this coincidence would have people believe that magic was a gift from God."

I rub the collar on my neck. "A curse for some."

After classes, I change out of my hospital gown and into my gym clothes. Luis and I head towards the elevator that leads to the top of the building to the soccer field. Cameras are set up around the field, so anyone wanting to watch can log in. There is no need for live spectators who can get hit by an errant blast of magic. I just *love* that they played the video of my last battle on the news. Three times. Some clever person had added in a laugh track. I won't find that funny for at least a month or two.

"See you next week," Luis says.

"Next week? What's that supposed to mean?"

"I just think you're going to take a day or two off, is all." Then he heads back into a stairwell that leads to the parking garage.

Emma isn't here to wish me luck. It must be her way of showing her disapproval. Marcus is here, though. And Val, the new girl.

The elevator's huge. Sometimes, they'd send over middle schoolers for testing, and we'd be crammed in there like a shipment of meat. It's just the three of us this time. When the middle schoolers came along, we called it a jamboree because of how many battles there were. Magical power gets revved up around the first year of high school. There are two magical career paths. Letting loose for energy in the power plants or fighting in the military. Since working in the plant is out of the question for me, I pursue my only other option. Very few people get picked because the armies are all androids now.

Of course, I could study hard like Emma or Luis, but that wouldn't lead to easy money after graduation. Most people work in the plant until their magic fades.

We reach the top of the building with a soccer field with faded white lines. The season ended a few weeks earlier, so nobody bothered to repaint it. A helicopter with a giant container attached to the bottom looms near the edge. An extensive set of empty metal bleachers stands on one side of the field, and a net encircles the top of the building to stop the ball or anyone from falling off.

"You ready, Jake?" Marcus asks.

"Still got my collar on, so nope. Someone'll have to take that off first."

He shakes his head. I don't think I've ever made Marcus laugh. Not for lack of trying.

"What did you get paired up against?" I ask Val.

She smiles. "I'm going up against you."

I believe her for a second, my mouth dropping open. Then I remember my assignment and try to play it off.

The helicopter was all black rather than the usual camouflage of military testers that visit the school. The different branches had blue, green, or urban camouflage on the truck. All black is new.

A colossal man leans on the truck. He wears a black suit that strains under the pressure of his muscles trying to burst out. He also wears a black tie and sunglasses. He has no military uniform, and he's solo. Usually, an officer and two other guys help with the bots if they malfunction.

"Good afternoon," the suited man says in the deepest voice I've ever heard. "I'm Agent Charleston. Thank you for coming to your evaluation."

"Agent? Agent for what?" I ask.

"D-O-G, Defense of the Globe," he says with a grin, rolling up his sleeve to show a tattoo of a snarling dog on his arm.

"Dumb name."

"Nobody asked you, little guy. First up: Marcus," the agent says.

Marcus walks up to the agent while Charleston takes out a collar remover. It looks like a stun gun. He sticks it onto Marcus' collar and pushes down on a button, and a loud zapping noise echoes across the field.

Marcus's collar falls to the floor with a clang, and he rubs his neck with one hand in the area where it had been. Everyone did it. It's an involuntary reaction. It felt like being reunited with a part of your body that'd been lost. The skin felt soft. Like brand new.

Agent Charleston picks up the collar and puts it on a small table. He retrieves a remote from his jacket and clicks a button. The side of the trailer under the helicopter rolls up to the top. Hundreds of bots sit on wracks like a walk-in closet. A small army slept in that container.

"Hate to break it to you kids, but the cameras are off, so all your little friends can't watch."

"How come?" The cameras on the poles that overlooked the fields didn't have their green blinking lights to show they transmitted the feed.

"With the Reds acting up, it's time for us to get more secretive about our defenses."

"Reds?"

"Martians."

"Oh, because they're from a red planet."

"No, because they're vampires that drink blood." I can't see his eyes behind those sunglasses, and he doesn't quite have the personality for it, but I imagine he fights back the desire to roll his eyes. "I have to apologize to you, Marcus."

"Why?"

"You aren't going to fight one bot with a 1,000 rating. You're going to fight a 1,000 with five more helping it."

"What? That's ridiculous. Nobody changes up the matches like that," I say.

"Sounds cool." Marcus grins like he's not surprised at all. As he heads out to the middle of the soccer field, he yells, "Let's go."

Charleston pushes a button on his remote. Metal clasps lower six bots out of the semi-truck.

Five are metal skeletons with something like motorcycle helmets, a dark black visor covering their faces. They stretch in unison, popping elbows and knees into the right place after storage.

The last one, though, has a different frame. It has an expressionless ceramic face and regular eyes. Plastic muscles cover the metal bones underneath. It scans its environment with a slow grinding of its head, probably seeing the world for the first time. It was just born.

Agent Charleston points his little remote right at Marcus. "Go!" The five metal skeletons sprint towards Marcus, who puts his knee out and leans to the side in a martial arts stance.

Just as the first skeleton gets to him, he leaps backward to reduce the momentum of the impact. They exchange punches and kicks before the next join in. And the next. Marcus deflects blows from three at a time. Three!

Then, the next two move around behind him, and there's only so much you can do when surrounded. He crouches down and then launches thirty feet into the air. He hovers there. He's flying.

Marcus can freaking fly.

CHAPTER 3: FIGHT LIKE A CARTOON

Marcus hovers above the bot skeletons that can only stand on the green field and stare up at their target. I'd heard that some fighters could fly. Androids too. I'd never seen it in person, though.

Agent Charleston bellows a deep and hearty laugh to himself. "I knew it. I knew he could do it."

I'm speechless. Actually, no, I'm not. "He couldn't do that even a month ago."

Val crosses her arms, the metal arm on top.

Marcus raises a fist, forming a purple aura around it. He throws a small ball of violet flames towards the ground in the space between the five bots. They scramble, running in different directions. He points at one of the retreating metal skeletons, and the ball races towards it instead of hitting the ground.

When the magic fireball hits its back, a small explosion blows the skeleton apart, sending metal fragments flying all over the grassy field. One of its hands, thin metal fingers splayed apart, lands next to me. I pick it up. "He wasn't nearly this powerful last month. How is this possible? Redirecting magic like that?"

"It's simple, Jake. Marcus is on another level than you," Val says.

"True. He's playing four-dimensional chess, and I'm still trying to get my first 'King Me' in checkers." I reach over to Val with the metal hand extended. "By the way, I haven't been acquainted with your metal self. Shake on it?"

She slaps the arm so hard out of my hand that it leaves an impression on the grass.

"Maybe later then," I say.

Marcus spreads his arms wide before throwing two more fireballs towards the ground. Each violet flame tracks one of the robots through the field before destroying them.

Agent Charleston points his remote up at Marcus, presses a button, and says, "Your turn."

The robot with a face spins its head toward the Agent. Glossy purple letters, 'X-53', shine on her chest. "Do I have to?" Its lips don't move when it speaks, and its voice carries the violent intent of a pacifist little twelve-year-old girl.

"Yes." Charleston points at Marcus. Again.

The robot runs in Marcus's direction. When she (I mean, I guess it's a she) gets about halfway, it leaps into the air, closing on him fast.

"Marcus, watch out!" I yell.

Too late. The bot lands a blow right to his face and sends him careening towards the net at the edge of the building. The net bends backward, and the beams lean outward but then fling him into the ground like a slingshot, the impact sending a small puff of dirt and dust into the air.

The two remaining metal skeletons circle around and pick up Marcus by the arms. His head is drooped down, clearly unconscious.

X-53 lands. Wait, she had been flying, too. She didn't just jump high. She puts her hands together, and a blue light emanates, forming a glow on Marcus's face.

"No!" I shout. Marcus can't defend himself or even stand by himself. The two skeletons were holding him up.

A blue ball of magical essence forms in the robot's hands. Way bigger than any I've ever seen. I get there in time just as X-53 nearly shoves the ball into Marcus. She turns her head towards me, her neck making a crick-crick-crick sound as it moves.

I slap the robot's clasped hands upward, sending the blue magic ball into the air. It explodes, the shockwave laying the grass down all in a direction outward from the blast.

X-53 cocks her head at about 45 degrees like a dog that had just heard a strange noise. "You tried to save him?"

"Yeah, of course."

"Interesting." X-53 punches me in the stomach. Air rushes out of my chest, and I can't suck any back in. With my collar still on, I don't have any magic to protect me. I crumple over onto the floor.

With my head buried in dirt and grass, I can still hear some struggling and two bangs. Metal shards land on me, some dropping in the grass right in front of my face. A WHOOSH follows another WHOOSH. I can finally suck in the slightest breath of air and roll over to face the sky.

Marcus trades a flurry of blows with X-53. He must've regained consciousness while I was down. It's difficult to watch them fight because they're so fast. It's just a blur of arms and legs. He lands a kick into the chest of X-53 that sends her plummeting towards the ground straight for Agent Charleston, who leaps out of the way just before she slams into the side of the helicopter instead.

The impact embeds X-53 about half a foot into the steel frame. She pushes against the metal door to get herself out. When she pops out, she leaves her shape in the passenger door. She stares up at Marcus, who's still flying in the air. She crouches down and flies right back up at him.

A purple aura surrounds Marcus's entire body. He lifts a hand and points it towards the oncoming robot. A violet beam shoots out from his palm and bursts straight through the robot's torso, melting the metal.

X-53 falls to the ground with a thud.

Marcus lands next to me. "Why did you do that?" He asks.

"You...needed help," I manage to say, arms clenched around my stomach.

He furrows his brow. "Never interfere with one of my fights ever again."

"Okay, geez." I hold up my hands in surrender.

Marcus walks to the helicopter, kicking a disembodied metal leg along the way. I prop myself up with an arm and kneel for a minute, catching my breath, before standing up. I march back, standing tall, trying to regain some dignity.

Marcus bows toward Charleston before the Agent snaps a collar back around his neck. Then Marcus leans against the truck and crosses his arms. The energy left his eyes. The collar locks away a part of him, caging it until the next time that someone from the military would take it off and set him free again.

Agent Charleston points at me. "Your turn. You ready?"

"Hell yeah!"

"Well, too bad. I just got an updated medical record for you. You've been in the hospital. Today even."

"So?"

"You're out. That's so. Val's going to take your spot for today."

Half of me fills with disappointment, my heart sinking a little. Relief fills the other half, like when someone cancels plans on you.

"I'm guessing she's not going up against what was on the board either. What is it? Two dozen bots? A giant bear prototype?" I ask.

"Dang, a bear. That's a promising idea. I'm gonna' pass that along." Charleston scratches his chin as if considering it. "Nah. Not a dozen. Not a bear. We're testing out a new wand and a different AI."

"A wand? So now the bots are a bunch of wizards? Got any potions, too, Agent?"

"W-A-N-D." Val spells it out for me. "A wave-altering neural device. It changes the way the magic works. Instead of pure energy, the wand changes the magic to something else. It's like the way the walls work except—"

"Except small enough for someone to hold," I say.

"Wear. You've got to wear it. Why don't you just wait a second? You'll see." Agent Charleston points his remote at the container underneath the helicopter and presses a few buttons. A metal claw lowers another bot.

"How do you know so much about this anyway?" I ask Val. She swats the air with her metal hand, batting away my question. I still want to know, so I'll push her buttons to get it out of her sooner or later. Never underestimate the annoying persistence of Jake Ryder.

"You got kicked out of the military, didn't you? Did you pick a fight with someone above your level? That how you got yourself chromed up?"

Val glares at me. It's the kind of face you never wanted to be on the receiving end of, with her eyebrows crashing down and a twitch of disgust. She makes me want to crawl out of my skin. "They'll take me back," she says.

Looks like I pushed the right button.

The bot finishes unloading from the truck. It moves its limbs and fingers in a rhythmic pattern, diagnosing itself. It has a plastic face, emotionless just like the last one, only this one's plastic skin and muscles are black. Cracks spread through its face, and the mouth twists into a sadistic grin. Its chest plate reads "Z-94".

Its right hand's different, and I haven't seen anything like it on a bot. A metal contraption overlays its hand and fingers, like a glove mimicking its movements. Each digit of each finger follows along.

"That the wand?" I ask, gesturing towards the bot's hand.

"You're a smart one," the Agent says.

"What's it do?"

"It's more fun for me to watch you figure it out. Come over here, Val. Let's get that collar of you."

"Don't need to," she marches to the middle of the grass field which adorned a faded logo of a lion, our school mascot. She must be insane. Without the collar on, she's a dead girl walking. You need your magic flowing. It helps even fighting with fists. For some reason, it changes the way physics affects your body. The strongest people, like Marcus (ugh), can be hit by a truck and still survive. I hate him. Even now, he's just silent, playing it cool.

"Okay," she yells. "Activate your tin can."

Agent Charleston nods at her from across the field. He points his remote at her, and a red laser glimmers below her neck.

Val doesn't even get into a fighting stance. She just stands straight up. What is she doing?

Z-94 jogs in her direction. "PREPARE TO DIE, SALINATED VERTERBRATE!"

"This one's spicy. Needs to work on its smack talk. Does it have to yell like that, though?" I ask Charleston. He shrugs.

Val doesn't flinch. She stretches out her metal arm at the bleachers, and they vibrate, screws and bolts coming out. How can she do that? One of the bleacher seats levitates into the air. She stretches out her hand at the droid. The metal beam zooms to Z-94 and impales through its chest, the long, shiny bleacher sticking out both sides.

"But how?" I ask.

Charleston grins. "Her prosthetic arm is a wand, too."

She launches bleacher beam after beam at the droid in a never-ending barrage. One knocks off its arm and another its leg. It tries to dodge to the side, but Val would spin the beam midair, turning it horizontal rather than as a piercing missile.

Val had used magic while still wearing her collar, and that is impossible. It must be broken. She didn't feel any pain when she missed class earlier. I've got to know how she does it. How did she free herself?

Z-94's just a floating chest piece with a beam pierced in the middle and a head still attached. Electricity flows all around it, and a buzz fills the air. Val finishes him with the one last beam, knocking its head clear. Metal shards and beams from what used to be the bleachers are scattered all over the place—a heck of a mess.

"I'm not cleaning this up." I pick up one of the fragments and toss it into a pile of rubbish.

Agent Charleston strides out to the middle of the field and picks up a disembodied hand, the glove still attached. "Yes, you are."

"How are you gonna make me do that, exactly?"

"The same way we do anything. A deal. You clean this mess up, and I let you try this out." He uses the droid hand to wave at me. It bends at the wrist with every swipe like a skeleton arm.

I wiggle my fingers, and my eyes light up. "Oh, we have a deal."

CHAPTER 4: THREE HUNDRED FIFTY QUINTILLION GALLONS

"What are you waiting for? Come over here so I can take off your collar," Agent Charleston says.

I obey like a good little dog, sauntering with my tongue out and tail wagging. He deactivates my collar, and it falls to the floor.

My body pulses with energy. I love this moment and wish I could be in this forever. It starts deep within my chest, like a jittery energy bouncing around my heart, like I just drank an extra-large sugary latte. From there, the feeling flows into my arms and legs. Then it intensifies in surges, waves of power rolling over and over, crashing onto the shore of my body.

"You okay? You look kinda like a psycho." Charleston's voice snaps me out of it.

My fists are clenched, my mouth in a twisted grin, and my eyes wide. Yeah, I can see how the Agent would make that connection. All I need is an evil laugh to finish the whole look.

"Gimme," I say. My hands clap together like two greedy crab claws, and I lurch toward the magical glove.

"I can't trust someone that looks like you right now."

"I'm just messing around. See." I pack my excitement away and stop smiling like a villain about to press a doomsday button. He fits the wand over my left hand. I wiggle my fingers, and each metal finger mirrors my actions. "Cool."

"Now, to use it, just—"Charleston's about to give me some sort of lecture, but I just sat through those all day. It's time for some fun.

I stretch my hand out at the pile of debris just like if I were to blast it. "No, wait!"

Too late. The whole pile of scraps tears through the net that surrounds the roof. A cacophony of crashes and loud scraping sounds echo from the street below. We all spring to the edge and peer over to survey the damage.

Drivers blare their car horns. Traffic piles up across several blocks. Water shoots up out of a water hydrant like a geyser.

"Is now a bad time to ask if I can keep this?"

"You're lucky I'm going to let you live. Give me that." Charleston grabs my arm, and he has the wand off of me in a flash. "Get outta here."

Marcus, Val, and I march back onto the elevator. The sun hovers just above the horizon now. Val rests her head against the wall, trying to relax.

"You always this great in the evaluations?" she asks.

"I know. I'm quite a specimen." I really want to change the conversation. "How'd you break your collar?"

"I told you, it's not broken."

"Then how do you do that?" There's a long, awkward silence as she gives me an icy stare. "I'll figure it out."

"No, you won't."

At the bottom, I say bye to Val and Marcus. Val doesn't move. Marcus salutes me. "Nice job today," he says.

"Very funny."

He returns this quizzical look. I mean, is he not sarcastic or cracking a joke? This dude's, I swear, just the weirdest. "I wasn't talking to *you*," he corrects.

The after-school buses still idle at the bus loop, and I ride one home. I have been living with Emma and Aunt Gracie, my mother's sister, since I was a kid. I have a makeshift bedroom formerly used for laundry. It gets hot as balls here, but I put in an air-conditioning unit myself last year. Aunt Gracie has yet to notice, though I'm sure I did some damage to the electricity bill. A mattress lies on the floor and not much else. This way, I can leave any second. Off to something better. The moment some uniformed people could show up at the front door and offer me a military commission out of here. A small window, filled mainly by the air conditioner, and some books. The real kind, made of paper. They don't make these anymore.

My left bicep aches just from using the wand for a second. I can't believe I'm saying this, but…I might be too tired to eat. Too many steps. Off to the kitchen to scrounge around for something. Forget it. Nothing here I like. I'll just eat this entire bag of chips.

Usually, Emma asks me how my evaluations go, but she hasn't stopped by yet. I collapse onto my floor mattress.

👍

The glaring light from my now-open door pierces through my crusty eyelids. My body rocks from side to side as some evil demon rocks me, saying, "Wake up!"

"Am I late for school again?" I ask.

"No, it's Saturday," Emma says.

"Waking me up early on a Saturday is the eighth deadliest sin. It's so bad that they don't even talk about it. Just the first seven."

"I was thinking we could go to the ocean today."

"Don't you have to work at the plant?"

"No. I have today off."

"Sure, then just give me six more hours."

"Get up. I'm leaving in thirty minutes."

"Go without me."

"Val, that new girl, is going to go."

I bolt upright. I have to learn from her how to bust out of my collar. "Let's get something to eat first, I'm starving."

Emma laughs. "I thought you might have a crush on her, but not *that* much of a crush."

"I don't. It's just that she has a secret, and I will figure it out."

"Sure. Whatever you say."

"Why'd you invite her anyway?"

"She was in one of my classes yesterday. I've been the new one in town before. I was a little surprised she agreed to come along." We get our swimming clothes on and throw a pile of towels into the trunk of Emma's strawberry wagon. We picked up Val at her house on the rich side of town, and after the first exchanges of pleasantries, there's this awkward silence during the car ride. I'm sitting in the front seat, Val in the back while Emma drives.

"You're a terrible fighter," Val snaps the silence in half.

"You're a terrible kisser," I say. The part of my brain that filters my thoughts with what I say takes a lot of breaks. She holds up her hands. *What?* I don't know what I was trying to go for there, either. Whitty retort fail. "I haven't had much practice fighting. I'll get better, you watch."

"No. Disregarding your magic. You just have bad form. Does your collar stop you from doing any physical training?"

"Maybe." It doesn't.

"You wind up when you punch," Val continues. "Way back. Like you're trying to high-five a gorilla. Anyone can see it coming and deflect it, block it, or anything they want."

"How are you supposed to do it?" I turn to face Val in the backseat.

Her fist barrels into my nose. Lightning fast. Bam! A blanket of darkness and stars fill my vision.

"Like that," Val says.

Emma screams and nearly loses control of the car.

I laugh, grab some napkins tucked away in the car door, and plug the new double bloody faucet that my nose has become.

"Why'd you do that?" Emma asks.

Val doesn't answer. She doesn't need to.

"Do it again," I say, spinning back around.

Val moves her fist directly from where it lay in her lap, right into my face. That's how to punch. No wind-up. Whap! This time in the cheek. I sit facing forward again, laughing. I'm learning more in a split second than I've ever learned in class. Cheek throbbing, the taste of warm blood pooling in my mouth. My tongue scrapes the sides of my teeth, checking for any loose ones. I never thought about the technique of fighting before. I just copy cartoons. Big wind-up punches look so badass though. Guess I have a lot to learn.

"You're so messed up," Emma says.

"Teach me how to use my whole body to punch like you later, okay?" The words resonate in my sinuses and sound like a nasal dork speaking. That describes me adequately.

About thirty minutes of driving later, we're almost there. One hundred feet high, a massive wall of water climbs over the horizon like a giant wave but without a white crest. Colossal pillars course with magilectricity that forms the transparent wall of pure energy. The pillars are like big metal tires stacked one on the other. The engineers created the modular design to stack more on top as the ocean level rose. It's as high as it would be since we had more ice in our freezer now than at the poles.

"It's impressive every time," I say.

"It goes underground, too, to stop the water from seeping underneath." Emma knows everything.

The magilectric plant sits in front of the wall. A big, square, concrete building with thick wires coming out all over the place. It plugs directly into the wall to generate the field that holds back the ocean. A few hundred people around my age sit in there right at this moment, collars off, pouring their energy into the plant. The energy of the young holds back the most tremendous deluge since the stuffing of a bunch of animals into a boat.

"How do I look?" I ask, pulling the red-stained napkin away from my nose.

"Like you got punched in the face," Emma says.

"Twice," Val says.

"Good thing school pictures are Monday," I say, grabbing a few of the beach chairs.

Val picks up the rest of the chairs, easily, and then picks up a cooler with two of her fingers. She's not even grimacing or struggling at all. "Believe it or not, it's an improvement over your usual self," she says.

"Wow, you've known me for two days and already with low blows like that."

"You're an easy target."

"You know, I think we're going to get along. But only if you can take it back."

"I can take a punch," Val says.

"Stop flirting," Emma says.

"If that was flirting, then it was the worst. Ever," I say. They agree.

A tall see-through tube rises to meet the top of the ocean's wall. That's where people get out to swim at the beach, basically floating platforms with sand on them.

"What's that?" Emma asks.

A colossal whale and its small calf float at the center of the wall on the ocean side. They hardly move except for a slight flick of their tails occasionally.

"Wow, that's amazing! I've never seen anything like it. I thought they were extinct. I want to get close," Emma says.

"It's on the way to the top. You'll see it when we ride up the elevator," Val says.

"The elevator's so fast, though. We'll hardly get a look at it."

"I have an idea." I always do.

We get into the elevator, a glass room connected to the outside of one of the pillars, and I hold my thumb over the emergency stop button.

"Don't. You're going to get us arrested or something," Emma says.

"We'll be fine."

As the elevator rises, I watch the whale and push the emergency stop just before we reach it. The elevator stops just level with the baby whale's eye, the size of a giant plate.

"What's your emergency," a voice says over the little speaker.

"This is," I say, tapping the elevator inspection notice, which has the name of an inspector, "Mr. Pearlman, I was just having a quick look at this unit and forgot to put in my master code."

"Okay, please remember in the future," the voice says.

"Will do."

The small whale shifts as close as possible to the force wall. Its skin presses flat against the surface.

Emma places her hands against the wall and peers into its eye. She's spellbound. The whale bellows a long, low song that shakes inside our chests. Emma turns around with a face that says *did you hear it?* How could we not?

White scars cover the mother whale's body, and crusty barnacles run along its underbelly. All those little ugly critters benefit from the whale and give nothing in return. It reminds me of all the young people in power plants, getting drained, mainly for the benefit of everyone else.

"We are the whale," I say.

"What the hell does that mean?" Val asks. Standing near two girls in their swimsuits, I should be more aware of drawing comparisons to large fat mammals.

"No, I just meant that—" Before I could finish, hundreds of small streams of water shot through the wall and rained down towards the ground. "What's happening?" I ask.

Emma spins around away from the whale. "The wall's failing. The whole ocean's going to come in!"

CHAPTER 5: THEY ARE THE BARNACLES

More and more holes blast out of the wall, and seawater streams toward the ground like someone poked hundreds of holes into a giant water balloon. A saltwater pond has already formed at the bottom, and it will overtake the parking lot before long.

"Oh my God, what do we do?" Emma asks.

Val points to the elevator buttons. "Up, up, up! Go up!"

I slam the emergency stop button again, and we shoot upward, our bodies lurching from the acceleration. A hole forms near the baby whale, and the outgoing water pulls the creature in. The whale pumps its tail up and down but still can't get away. The mother lets out a long, low cry.

"We've got to do something," Emma says, her voice quivering.

We got out of the elevator and leaned over the edge. Vast pillars of water are already pouring out..

"It's not going to hold," Val says. "We've got to power the pillars."

"How? We've got these on." I point to my collar.

"Just come with me."

We speed along the top platform that connects the pillars to the column of metal tires that conducts the magilectricity. Bolts of magic skitter up and down the open center, dance in circles, but then dim and putter out before starting up again.

"What's wrong with it?" I ask Emma.

"I don't know. It could be low on power, or the whole pillar is malfunctioning," she replies.

Darkness spreads from the top to the bottom of the pillar, and the wall almost completely powers down. A deluge of water crashes down, and the baby whale is lost somewhere in the churning white foam. The wave carries away cars parked in the lot and continues down the road. The mother whale's too big to fit in any developing holes, but her worried song echoes inside my head.

"Holy crap." I lean over the side railing to get a better view.

"Oh no!" Emma screams and reaches down as if she could pull the whale from the watery maelstrom.

The plant's nearby, and the water rises quickly in the area around it. "If the plant floods, then this whole wall section could go out," I say.

"Come on." Val extends her right arm toward the dark gap in the column and unleashes a beam of red magic. It splits apart like light through a prism, changing to distinct colors and bouncing down to the bottom. Despite whatever Val's trying to do, the wall still isn't turning back on.

"I'm not enough. You need to do it, too," Val yells to me. The torrent of water crashes through the gap in the pillars. It's so loud we have to shout at each other. She keeps firing nonstop, but what she's doing is impossible. Her collar must be frying her neck off.

"How?" I ask. "How do you do that?"

"Power up just like when the collar's off." She grimaces. "It hurts like hell. You just have to concentrate."

I stretch out a hand towards the column's center. Concentrate, huh? Where is that energy at anyhow? It comes out so quickly when the collar's off. It builds up in my chest while searing pain flares in my neck, proportional to the amount of energy I build.

The energy piles up, and I lose focus, again and again, until just powering through the pain. I can't help but scream. I can't be embarrassed. Nobody can hear me over the waterfall anyway. Enough energy gathers in my hand that now a blue aura surrounds it, the pain around my neck so intolerable that it's hard to breathe, like my collar chokes and shocks me at the same time. It feels like my breaths are being sucked in through a straw.

A powerful magical current flows from me, the lights of different colors twirling into a long ribbon of a beam, but it's exhausting. I'm not used to unloading in a constant stream like this. Emma's doing her best, but her magic barely trickles out. Her face contorts and twists from the pain. Val's reddened face is her only sign of duress.

The wall slowly regenerates from our side before connecting back to the other column. The torrent of water stops.

The pain from the collar's unbearable. I take a break. "Whew. That's tiring and worse than touching a fire." Almost immediately, the wall dissipates again, streams of water flying out. "Oh God, I don't know how long I can keep this up."

"The repair team should be here soon," Val says. "Don't stop now." After a five-minute eternity, three helicopters fly in, each carrying a stack of metal pillar tubes. We move out of the way, and they stack their replacement parts on top of the broken pillar while tech teams remove the malfunctioning bits. The elevator has survived the flood since we left it at the top, and we ride it down to the bottom.

Emma runs over to the whale. The calf lies on its side, breathing laboriously, and can't move in only a few inches of water. Its mother floats at the ocean's surface back at the wall, spouting water into the air and moaning in long, low songs.

"Can't you help it?" Emma asks one of the tech responders.

With a collar around his neck, the responder can't be much older than us. "No, sorry. It's too heavy. We'd need a helicopter and a special sling to ensure we don't kill it." He turns his back to the whale, takes out his phone, and snaps a selfie with a big grin. Jerk. If he posts that anywhere, I hope he takes flak from all his friends and family.

Emma kneels by the calf, touching its head just above the eye. "We have to do something. Anything," she says. It arches its back, lifting its fluke into the air, but it doesn't make any noise.

Val and I stand out of earshot from Emma. "We're the whale, eh?" she asks.

I shrug. I can't control every word that comes out of my mouth. "Yes, and they are the barnacles."

"They?"

"Can you lift it up over the wall? Using your fancy glove thingy."

"Heck no. That thing is huge. I've never lifted anything so heavy. And that wall is at least fifty feet tall. Probably more."

I glance over at the elevator. "What about ten feet?"

"That'll never work."

"We can't just sit here and watch two hearts break." I gesture to Emma, and the mother whale is still patrolling on the other side of the transparent levee.

"Fine. I'll lift it off the ground, and you help push it closer." Val holds her hand out at the whale with her fingers spread like she has an invisible plate. The calf lifts an inch off the ground, and I push it toward the elevator with my hands sinking into the fatty flesh. Its skin is leathery and slimy at the same time. Val sets it down right next to the lift. "You ready?" she asks.

"Me? What am I gonna' do?"

"Help me lift it, tough guy. Let's go."

I put my fingers underneath the baby whale, ready to lift. Its huge eye stares into my soul like it knows I'm trying to help. "Ready."

"Okay. Go!" Val grimaces as her metal arm vibrates. I can't imagine how much pain she's in. I try to help lift the infant leviathan, but it's too heavy. My legs shake, and my knees ache. When the whale's two feet off the ground, I get underneath and try squatting it into the air. My collar singes me as I summon the strength to help.

The whale rises over seven feet up, and I can barely reach it with my arms, the tips of my fingers slipping off its rubbery, wet skin. Val has to take it the rest of the way. Small tributaries of red magic flow over her, forming into bigger bands and coursing toward her arm. Her face blushed as she bared her teeth. Her collar glows with heat.

She gets the whale to the top of the elevator. Its head and tail hang over the sides.

"You...are amazing," I say to Val.

"I know." She wiggles the mechanical fingers, and they screech as they move. "Not sure this'll work anymore."

Emma climbs to the top of the elevator. "I'll keep it calm. Get it going, Jake." She pets the top of its head and whispered to the animal.

Val and I board the elevator, heading down. The red warning light blinks as we lifted into the air. Slowly. A loud grinding emanates from the lift's mechanisms. After we reach the top, Val lifts the whale just a bit, her arm shaking violently, and I give it one big push, sending it into the sea with a splash.

The mother whale torpedoes over and pushes its baby back up to the surface. Both marvelous creatures are singing.

"They look happy." Val crosses her arms and smirks.

"They're saying thank you," Emma says. "Jake, are you crying?"

"Nope, definitely not. Just some seawater that got on my face."

Aunt Gracie gives us a ride home. It's pitch black out now. Talk about a long day. Emma falls asleep in the car on the way back to Tallahassee.

"Sounds like you're all heroes," Aunt Gracie says with her hands on the wheel. *10 & 2*, she always says while teaching us. Not that learning how did me any good.

"Only you can prevent the aquatic apocalypse," I say.

Val just shrugs. Like what we did is no big deal. "It depends on if the plant would've shut down or not. If it would have then, yeah, we saved the day. Otherwise, the tech team showed up pretty fast."

"Why would they build the plant so close to the wall? It's dumb for exactly this reason," I say.

"The wall wasn't always there." Aunt Gracie drives onto Capital Circle, the busiest highway in the city. "It used to be closer to the original shoreline, but that whole line failed. Gosh, that was a long time ago. I think my grandmother was just a kid when that happened."

"Wish we had more of a backup plan. That sure seemed close," I say.

"There aren't enough metals left to build more magilectric pillars for backup plans," Val says. "That's why this whole thing with Mars is such a big deal. We need the asteroid belt to keep our walls up. They need the asteroid belt to build their new cities."

"We've got armies of droids. Pretty sure we'll win if anything starts up," I reply.

"Probably."

Val's huge house has perfectly trimmed hedges, a rose garden, and a gate stopping us from entering. What do her parents do for money? Not that she'd ever tell me. Val's a black hole of her own past. Each moment goes into her and then never comes back out. She hops out of the car and we all say bye. I roll the window down. "Hey Val, will you teach me to fight?"

She walks backwards towards the door while talking. "What do I get?"

"A friend?"

She laughs. "You'll have to try harder than that."

"I *am* trying," I yell before she closes the front door.

For the second day in a row, I fall asleep instantly. Wham, face meet pillow, brain meet darkness.

The next day, the mirror tells a story on my face. The bruises have ripened nicely after getting socked by Val in the face. Emma sits on the couch in the living room, which has giant tears in it that we covered with duct tape. She's watching the news.

"How do I look?"

"Like an eggplant." Emma smiles.

"Good. My favorite vegetable." Not really. More of a carrots guy. Wait, do potatoes count as a vegetable? Them then. If not, carrots. I sit down next to Emma.

"Is it really? I think they're disgusting."

"No, my real favorites are tomatoes." Okay, so I changed my mind.

"Tomatoes are a fruit."

"Same thing. They're both on my zero servings per day diet."

On the TV, two people in suits talk energetically, their words coming out so fast that their words mix together into one nonsensical babble. "What's going on in the world today?" I ask.

"We made the news."

"What? Like, big time TV?" I sit up straight. "That's amazing. Did they show footage?"

"Well, we were *on* the news. There have been a lot of failures. Los Angeles had a bad scare yesterday, too. They had a foot of saltwater in downtown."

I'm picturing people floating on the letters for the Hollywood sign. Emma continues, "The World President declared a national emergency, and lots of Governors did, too. Mandatory plant duty for all collar-aged people."

"Holy crap, that's a big deal."

"Yeah, they're talking about whether it's moral or not," Emma says while gesturing to the two talking heads on TV. "They're making some good points. There isn't a difference between this and drafting us to go to war for them. At least this way, we don't die."

"None of that is okay. They're taking something from us just because we're alive. On the bright side. Though Mom can't possibly be upset at me for working there if it's an order from the President. Maybe I can buy my own car."

"True."

"And I'm tired of riding into school via your trunk. It's hurting my game. You know. With the ladies."

"You'd need more than a car to fix that. Like a whole new personality. And there's no used dealership for that."

"Nice one. If there were, though, what should I get? Rich college boy home for spring break?"

My phone rings. After a brief conversation, I hang up and take a deep breath.

"What was that all about?" Emma asks.

"I'm going to prison."

CHAPTER 6: SOCIETY WRAPPED AROUND THE NECK

I have a recurring daydream where I bust Mom out. I've visited the prison enough times that I know the layout by heart. In the fantasy, I go in like on any routine visit, but in the long hallway to the visiting room, I blast away the two bots standing guard. There's no bot in the place with a power rating over 100. I can do it. Then, the glass that separates the visitors and the prisoners melts under one of my blasts. My Mom jumps over the divider through shards of glass, and we run back down the hallway. Other prisoners and visitors would scatter in the chaos, causing even more confusion while Mom and I get out of there. But once we would escape, what would we do? Get caught and die. That's what.

In the real world, I'm riding an automated taxi to the edge of Tallahassee. Towers rise from each corner of the prison, with two droids standing as stoic guards at the top. There is no need for entertainment—they have constant vigilance against escapees or attempts to break them out.

The visiting room has a chalkboard titled "Today's Contraband." A stapler is number five on the list. I can't imagine it being an effective escape weapon, so some prisoners must be into crafts or paperwork. Inmates don't have to speak through a phone, so slipping them a package might be possible, but my Mom is not one of them. I sit down on my usual stool in front of the dividing glass. Mom already has a phone to her ear. Dark circles drape beneath her eyes, and her whole face sags down. They drained all the hope from her. It makes me feel awful seeing her this way. The escape fantasy replays quickly in my mind.

That's not to say I love my Mom like other people do. I don't have a single memory of Mom being a mom if that makes sense. She's been locked up my whole life. Still, there sits a woman that I care about, and each time I see her, her whole body loses more and more of the life within.

"Mom."

"What happened to your face?"

"You should see my opponent."

"Pummel him good, did you?"

"Nope. And he's a she."

"I'm glad Emma's got some help putting you in your place."

"Thanks."

"How's school?"

"Fine." I don't know why I'm being short with her. I don't know if I'm upset at her, myself, or the whole world. I wish I could stop and appreciate the time I can spend with her, but I can't.

"Are you working on any projects? Studying hard?"

"Negatory."

"What are you going to do after you graduate?"

"Military."

"They are *never* going to take you. Ever. Do you think they're going to take the son of two rebels? Oh, sorry, they call us terrorists."

"Rather than this becoming another visit where we fight, why don't you tell me why I had to come here? What couldn't you say over the phone?"

"I wish you had a sister. I need someone a bit more sensitive to visit me every once in a while."

"I'm very sensitive. I even have a special toothpaste for it."

"Always a jokester. That's good. It'll carry you through some tough times."

"Tough times? Like growing up without parents? Being the only person at school who doesn't work at the plant to please his dead father's wishes? How many girls are interested in a sixteen-year-old without a car or money?"

"You can't be the only—"

"Yeah, I'm the only one."

Silence replaces our conversation. A faint buzz of static fills my ear, and the unintelligible discussions of the other guests fill the other. Mom looks up at the clock and then speaks. "Listen, about the plant."

"I've avoided working there, and now I *have* to do it. Otherwise, they might lock me up in here with you."

"Jake, sit close."

"Why? We're talking over a phone. It's not like you can whisper to me through the glass."

"Just do it."

I shift as close to the glass as possible without pressing my face against it. Mom hunches forward, stares at her closed fist like it holds a secret, and furrows her brow.

A faint blue glow forms around her fist. She opens it up and faces her palm upwards. A blue flame flickers there before she closes her hand again, and then the magic dissipates.

"How? You're, like, twenty years past collar age."

She opens her hands again and summons a marble-sized orb that she passes between her fingers. "They drain your magic from you when you work at the plant. It has nothing to do with age. They use it all up. It's finite. That's what your father and I fought for back before they paid you to work there. Before, it was voluntary. Guess we're back to those days." She flicks her hand, and the magic disappears again.

"Slavery," I say.

Mom nods. "Indentured servitude. They called it 'earning your place'. Or, my favorite, a rite of passage."

This changes everything for me. The justification for taking our magic always goes something like: *it will fade away naturally anyhow. We might as well use it to save all these buildings that belong to the rich. Right?* Now I know they're taking it from us. They're about to steal it from *me*.

"So they just pay us a little money for our power?" I ask.

"That's right. Just the cost of preventing another revolution."

"What am I supposed to do? I'm not a rebel. Things didn't end up that great for you the last time around."

"If you can't snake your way out working at the plant, just do as little as possible. Especially on your first day. They'll try to measure your future performance from your first day."

"Okay. I'll see what I can do."

The guard droids usher the visitors out. "Gotta go."

"I know. Love you, Jake."

"Sure. Bye."

👍

Emma and I arrive at the plant in her replacement Strawberry Wagon (for once, an insurance company did the right thing) for my first day. I've been outside of the concrete monster of a power plant dozens of times. On each trip to the floating beach, it sits there, staring at me, making it impossible to relax completely.

"Ready?" Emma asks.

"What's it like in there?

Emma laughs. "You're just wondering about that now? Right before you go in?"

I hadn't thought about what it would be like on the inside. I always imagined it as an evil place. That's how my parents raised me, on stories of the turmoil and struggle inside.

"You'll like it, Jake. There are naked girls in there," Emma says as she exits the car.

"What?" I didn't ask anything else because she had to be kidding anyway.

The side of the building has two giant green doors for trucks and heavy equipment and two smaller doors for people, one marked with a boy and the other marked with a girl stick figure, like bathrooms. Each door has a plant employee with a hard hat and a white lab coat standing guard in front. Emma leads the way to the door on the left. The man by the door has a thick mustache and scans Emma's collar. "Welcome back, Emma."

"Bye, Jake," she says with a little wave and a smile. She fades away into the darkened hallway.

"Why? Aren't I going with you?" I ask. She's already gone too far to answer.

"First timer, huh? This is the girl's entrance." The mustache man bobs his head towards the other entrance, tilting his hard hat forward. "That there's for dudes."

"Why do you split us up?"

He smirks, his mustache arching upward. "You'll see. Go on that way."

A younger man scans my collar before I head inside. A black door waits at the end of the already dark hallway. This is a freaking power plant. Can't they have some lights? Past the door, rows and rows of metal lockers went through a large changing room with long wooden benches. My brief and unsuccessful tryouts for the soccer team had led me to believe that locker rooms needed to smell like fermented dude sweat caked onto polyester outfits. The power plant staff may clean the uniforms every day.

Some other guys are already taking off their shoes. Luis Gonzalez clicks his boots together and stares at a dim light from the ceiling. "Hey, good to see you on the same shift as me," I say.

"Funny seeing you here. Total newbie. You are going to sleep well tonight," he says, a faint glimmer in his eye as if he knows a joke that I don't.

"Is there an outfit we put on or what?" I ask.

"Sure, there is. You're wearing it."

"Oh, okay, so there's not a uniform. Then why is there a locker room?"

"There's a uniform. We all wear the same thing. Nothing." He smiles.

"Are you serious?"

"Yep. It's to maximize your surface volume with the magilectric absorption pads on the chair." He's just showing off now. "Don't worry, you get used to it."

This dream creeps into my sleep, uninvited, every so often. I'd show up to school without any clothes on. Or better yet, I'd walk around the hall with my zipper open and my Jocko hanging out, never noticing the breeze until someone stopped to point and laugh at me, everyone else joining in.

It's not a dream, though; the other guys are lining up near another black door, and they stand with their hands straight down to their sides. I join them awkwardly, trying my best to cover myself up.

"Oh, poor Jake," says Mark, a senior. "Embarrassed that you can't measure up with the rest of us?" Everyone laughs. Everyone. Even Luis.

"Nope. Just trying to keep you from getting jealous is all."

"Yeah, okay."

We're 'at attention' for an eternity before the door opens, and another man in a hard hat leads us down several hallways. Our bare feet slap against the cold floor, making the most bizarre marching sound, like a bunch of people rhythmically flopping pancakes on plates.

There's another room marked "Extraction Chamber 3C". It's like a movie theater with rows of strange chairs all facing forward, except they all face a pane of glass instead of a screen. Behind the glass, another plant employee sits behind a large console filled with glowing dials, buttons, and controls.

A little screen flickers on the back of a chair reading "Jacob Ryder." Assigned seating? The chair leans back only a little. I can't quite get my true Jake lean on, but the material's like sitting on two cold granite slabs. Restraints automatically slide out of the armrests and strap down my arms. Four more wrap around my ankles and thighs. A final one closes around my forehead and pins my head to the chair.

The restraints are tight and firm, and breaking out is impossible, even without a collar: a loud snap and my collar disengages.

The person in the lab coat behind the glass holds up five fingers. Then four. Three. Two. Then he slaps a lever up on the console.

I jolt in the chair. "Oh God," I whisper through bared teeth. It feels like small flames licking all the skin on the chair. My power's surging out of my back. I can't control it at all, but then it comes back to me what Mom said. About how our magic might be permanent if we didn't get it all drained, and at this rate, I'd lose all my power after the first session. I have to hold it back somehow.

I squirm and ground my teeth together. Torture. This is torture. The only relief comes from relaxing and letting them take it all. Holding back the flow of magic feels like a full bladder, but only relieving yourself at a quarter the speed, all the while it stings.

Nausea takes over. Saliva swells in my mouth, and pressure builds up in my chest. My breakfast rises up and out, and I find a new home all over me.

Back in the locker room after it's finally over, I'm cleaning myself up when Mark says, "Thanks for not holding anything back in there, Jake. The aroma made this shift, uh, different." I glare at him. The witty center of my brain's off.

Clothes back on and smelling slightly better, I meet Emma in the parking lot. "How'd it go?" Emma asks.

"I can't do for much longer," I say.

"Oh, it's not *so* bad."

"It's that bad. I'm going to have to get out of it somehow."

CHAPTER 7: MONKORO FAMOUS

Things are great if greatness is a dingleberry on a dead buffalo. School. Training with Val and Marcus. Getting my soul sucked out of me three times a week for a few bucks. Auntie Gracie makes fun of me. She says she went to work five times a week at her office for the soul-sucking experience but gets paid less per hour than I do.

Val trains us inside an abandoned warehouse, but neither Marcus nor I progress much. He can already fly without his collar on, but the pain cripples him to the point where we're even. I improve my physical technique a lot, moving punches and kicks aside while landing my assaults on occasion.

Then Val has us meet her at the aqua shuttle. It's a train station where a massive hole forms in the middle of the ocean, and a tube pierces through the wall of water.

The station is pristine, with marble floors and ornate character-themed decorations. A cartoon mouse's head forms the door knobs. People from all over the country come here to ride to the island of Orlando. The theme parks there all banned together and created their own state. They power their own walls, holding back the surrounding ocean.

Marcus and I sit next to each other on two padded seats, waiting for Val.

"You got enough money for a ticket?" Marcus asks.

"Yeah, I work at the plant now, remember?"

"True, true."

Val's wearing shorts, exposing two long legs, one with ivory skin and the other a chrome metallic bar extending into a sneaker. I am better now and not staring, but sometimes it's like my eyes control themselves.

"You boys ready?" she asks.

"Not really. I was born *not* ready," I say.

"If you put ketchup on a cliché, it's still a cliché but with more condiments." Val gives me that smirk, meaning I should cut down on the jokes for the rest of the day.

"What are we doing anyway, Val?" I ask. "What can we do in Orlando for training that we can't do here?"

"You two are registered to compete in the Monkoro Open this weekend."

"Monkoro? Isn't that for dorks?"

"I don't think your level of cool qualifies you for bestowing that title on anyone. Anyway, you two will be competing with your collars on."

"So, we're sure to lose," Marcus says. If there's one thing Marcus and I have in common, it's that losing was to be avoided at all costs. There's no character-building or consolation prize when it comes to losing for either of us.

"Probably. But it will be a fun way for you guys to get out of your current funk and break through the pain barrier.

"Alright. Let's do it."

We hop onto the next shuttle. The long car zooms through a tunnel of glass piercing through the middle of the ocean's wall. If one of the windows cracks, then we'll all be dead. It's one of those comforting realizations that will make this two-hour ride no sweat at all. I kick my feet on an empty seat and stare out a window. It's disappointing that the ocean's dark even a few dozen feet below the surface. Though I still enjoy staring off into the never-ending aquamarine. Periodically, the shuttle gets close to the top or the bottom so you can better understand where you are. A little bit outside of Orlando, the shuttle passes a submerged skyscraper. It has lights all over it and giant spotlights pointed at the bottom of the sea.

"Woah," Marcus says. He presses his face against the glass. Val's disinterested, staring at the ceiling.

It's not like merpeople live in it, but they set it up as a memorial. Not to anybody that died, but to Earth as they knew it then. It's just an underwater building to me. We should stop torturing ourselves in the plants so that rich people can hold onto their buildings. We should worry about farmable land. We could keep up some of the magilectric walls for that, but there's no reason to imprison young people forever.

"Jake, snap out of it, we're here," Val says.

I'd been running my hands along my collar and not paying attention to the outside since we had passed the memorial building. "Right."

The station in Orlando has way more people, emphasis on way, and way more advertising. Throngs of people. Throngs? Sure, that's a word. Monitors and holograms glare with bright colors that grab our attention. Fastest ride in Orlando! 230 miles per hour! Meet your favorite cartoon! Bam! Bam! Bam! Give us your money. The joke's on them, though. I don't have much to give.

Droids, twenty feet tall, shaped in the image of famous characters, stomp through the streets. A giant mouse bends down to a group of children. "Hoo hoo, how about a slushy?" The kids cheer. The giant scans their collars for transactions, and then it poops out green goo into cups with metal claws handing them out to the children. I mean, okay? I'm never paying for a butt slushy.

Val leads us straight to the conference center. We pass the different theme parks and roller coasters towering into the sky. One ride goes up a mile high, and a cart full of people screams as it barrels down to the ground. Now that's awesome. *That* I want to do.

"Flying is better," Val says.

"I can't fly." I've seen Val do it several times while training with Marcus.

Val smiles. "Oh, but you will eventually.

A giant wall of water circles the entire city. The whole ocean presses down onto it to get in. This feels a lot more disturbing to me than back home. In Tallahassee, there's the illusion that if the walls fail, we can return further inland. Here, well, I hope you can swim, bud.

We pass tourists snapping pictures of each other and food vendor stalls, one after the next. A giant screen shows the news with no sound with a caption reading, "Tensions Rise with Mars".

"Hurry up," Val yells.

The conference center opens to an enormous space where hundreds of people mill around rows and rows of vendors selling their products. One stall custom paints Monkoro equipment. The main piece is a black helmet with two hanging wires connecting to the specialized chair, similar to one of the power plant chairs. The helmets let you create and control a 'condensed' hologram. A vendor paints the logos onto the sides of helmets belonging to a team of girls waiting nearby.

Marcus, Val, and I trek to the back. We're forced to walk past all the vendors, a setup that must be in the hopes of us spending money (yay, capitalism!). In a twist of fate, Luis is at a vendor stall with his brothers, and I split off from Marcus and Val without a word to say hi to him instead.

"Hey Luis, what's up with the stall? You selling snacks? I sure could go for a bagel right now."

Luis gives me a smile that says, *I know you're not that stupid*, then actually says, "My brothers and I have some projects and prototypes we're pitching to Monkoro developers and military types. Maybe somebody will pick one up or buy a patent from us."

"Like what? Whatchya got?"

Luis spins around and picks up a sword. "Like this. The metal draws in power from the wielder and strengthens it so it can't be broken like a normal weapon." If I used a normal weapon in a fight, it'd snap in half if the opponent was strong enough. Magic has basically ruined the laws of physics. Einstein's rolling in his grave. Which is underwater now, probably.

"Let me see." He hands me the sword. My collar zaps at my skin as I summon the strength to bend the blade in half.

"It's a prototype," Luis says.

"Keep working on it. If anyone can figure it out, it's you."

"Jake!" Val calls from across the giant conference room. "Hurry up!"

"See you later, Luis."

"Sure thing."

Over at the pre-trials, they evaluate our talents at Monkoro and place you in a league. I've seen some videos, so I know roughly how this works, but this is my first time playing it. The equipment alone is too expensive. It's like a rich kid's game. The chairs are exactly like the ones in the power plant, but the armrests are the only metal to absorb magic lines. They draw our power from the forearms to create the monster, standing maybe three or four inches tall, which appears on a table between the two contestants. Then, the monsters battle to the death. Or whatever, they aren't alive. Right?

Right?

Marcus sits down first across from some kid, a girl who can't be older than eight. A woman with a badge on her chest asks Marcus, "May I take off your collar now?"

He shakes his head, and his large puff of hair trails his motion. "Nah."
The woman flips a switch. Marcus grits his teeth as the chair draws power
from him.

The little kid instantly summons up a four-armed creature, swords in
each hand. It spins its swords in circles.

Marcus struggles and stares at the board. Slowly, a tiny, four-legged
rodent appears without any fur. Or teeth. Or anything. I'm not sure how
Marcus expects it to fight.

It doesn't.

The four-armed creature walks over and kicks the rat off the board. Just
like that, Marcus is done. He gets up from his chair, rolling his neck, the
pain of his collar still fresh. "That was tough."

"Yeah, you can see why I wanted you guys to do this," Val says. "It'll
be a good training exercise. You'll do better after they place you in the
Green League. That kid there is pretty good."

The woman with the badge walks over to me. "You're up."

The mop-haired kid still sits in the chair. She's very pale. A beast with
three heads of a lion, dragon, and goat forms a logo on her shirt. A weird
school mascot?

"I'm facing her too?" I ask. The woman nods. I sit in the chair, the steel
feeling hot as it presses to my forearms. Just a little time with Marcus had
heated it quite a bit.

"Collar off?" the woman asks as she leans toward me with the collar
key. Everyone except Marcus has had their collars removed.

"You gonna' be terrible just like your friend?" the little girl asks.

"What?"

"I'm going to beat you in…less than three seconds." She grins like the
Cheshire cat.

Do I plan on losing to this little brat? I think not. "Collar off," I say to the badged woman. Val glares at me with a red face that could melt a snowman in a blizzard. I know this ruins the whole point of the training, but I have to kick this kid's butt. Mind monsters or otherwise.

"Okay," the badged woman says. She takes off the collar. I feel the skin on my neck. Puffy. Wrinkled. Scarred and torn from using magilectric powers with the collar on during training. I'd wear a collar for life, whether it was made of metal or my own scarred skin.

"I'm ready," I say.

The woman flips the switch, and a hum travels through the chair. It is similar to the power plant but way less potent. Within a moment, the mop-haired kid summons up her four-armed creature again, spinning swords back and forth.

"Let's see what you got," the kid says.

I grin. "All right. Here's what I got." I squint at the table, concentrating, forming my energy and thoughts into one. I picture a black creature with tentacles, mouths, and eyeballs floating around like a demonic octopus blob. I have no idea where this is coming from. It forms, growing bigger and bigger, as I imagine on the table. It grabs the girl's four-armed creature without a problem.

"What?" The kid can't believe it.

I laugh. It's just so easy. I can roll right through these. I've finally found something I'm way better at than Marcus. They'll place me in the highest league, and I'm going to be a freaking champion. Worldwide Monkoro famous.

The black blob grows increasingly, tentacles growing longer and thicker until it fills the space between the two chairs. It's not supposed to get that big, and I can't control it anymore.

"Make it stop," says the badged woman.

"I can't. I can't control it."

She moves towards the lever, but the monster slips a tentacle around her, squeezing her arms to her side. It's getting larger and larger, wrapping tentacles around me and keeping my arms forcibly attached to the chair, feeding it more power. Reaching ten feet tall, dozens of eyes coalesce over its round frame. Two of them droop down and peer right into mine. A mouth full of jagged teeth opens beneath what I can only call a smile.

A monster is born.

And I'm its daddy.

CHAPTER 8: FROM ONE MONSTER TO THE NEXT

The tentacles slither all over the convention hall, picking up tables, chairs, and even people, grabbing them by the legs as they run away and then scooping them into the air.

Marcus and Val dodge their way to safety. "Guys! You've got to hit me with all that you've got to stop this thing," I yell.

Marcus puts his hands at the sides of his mouth to make a little megaphone, "That'll kill you."

One tentacle whips around a man, squeezes him tightly, and purple fills his face. "You don't have a choice," I yell back. "Do it!"

Val and Marcus nod at each other and sprint toward me, ducking under and jumping over tendrils as they whip across the room. They aim their open palms in my direction.

"Sorry, dude," Marcus says.

"Just do it, you wimp."

I peek a single eye open. The glowing magic was building in their hands. This is going to hurt.

A lot.

When their blasts hit, my head whips back, and the monster lets loose a sound like a thousand eagles gargling. I grip the chair's armrests, but it changes from hardwood into flaky, crumbling pieces like a rotten log before disintegrating entirely. The right side of my face burns as if someone presses my face against the stove turned to the highest setting.

Then everything goes black.

☍

My head feels like it's split down the middle. An unfamiliar man's face hovers over me.

"Woah, angels sure are ugly," I say.

The man grunts and backs away from me. "He's alive," and then he walks away to help someone else. He's got on a paramedic's outfit.

"Did I win the tournament?" I grin at the nearest silhouette.

"No, and I'm pretty sure you won't be playing again. Ever," Val says.

"What happened anyway?"

Val shakes her head. "All I can say for sure is you have a monster inside you. A monster you don't know how to control. We'd better get out of here before Orlando police get here and put you in a psychiatric ward. Or the military gets here and puts you in a research lab."

Both of those sound better than school," I say. Not really, though. I'd rather dissect a frog than be examined myself.

Val sighs and leads Marcus out of the conference center. I stand up and brush myself off. How wasn't I hurt more? Only the headache serves as my punishment. I touch the top of my head and feel the actual outcome. The hair on the right side of my head has burned away. My reflection in a window confirms my loss of hair.

All in all, it's not a bad look for me: angry Viking dude. Should've shaved off the mop a while back. Only know once you try, right?

I catch up to Marcus and Val. "I needed a haircut. Hope you guys don't mind if I pass on the tip this time." Sirens blare in the distance.

"Shut up, Jake. I told you to wear your collar," Val says.

"I wanted to win. So, what?"

"You just destroyed a Monkoro conference. You've just drawn a huge amount of attention to us." Val lifts her hoodie up over her head.

"What's wrong with a little publicity?"

"Some of us don't want to be found." Val points to her metal arm.

"Right, mysterious cyborg girl. You'll forgive me for not caring."

Val huffs and stomps faster towards the subways. Marcus stares at me blankly, a look that says something like, *you're better than that, man.* But am I?

I sigh and catch up with her. "Listen, I'm sorry. I didn't mean to summon up a giant person-eating squid thing. Okay? I have no idea what happened. I just wanted to win. That's all. That's why I had them take off the collar. I wanted it to be fair."

Val seems to accept this apology, at least partially. But then she opens her mouth, and whenever that happens, usually someone disagrees with me. "Yes, but it's not fair. These are normal kids. We're training to—" she stops for a second, staring off into the distance, "—not be normal." Then she opens and closed her metal hand several times, flicking the artificial fingers up and down.

We board the shuttle and sit in silence with Val, pissed, embarrassed, and Marcus, well, he hardly ever says or expresses anything.

The screens on the trains change from some boring talk show to "BREAKING NEWS." A video feed from the huge mining space station out in the asteroid belt comes through, with an announcer talking the viewers through it.

The space station glows brightly from the inside. Then explosions light up every corner of the station.

"Holy crap," Val says. "They actually did it."

"The Martians?" I ask.

"Yeah, them, who else?"

"How many people were on that station?" asks Marcus.

"Gotta be over ten thousand at least," Val says

"This is...this is all-out war, then? What will we do to respond?"

Val shakes her head and doesn't answer. We keep watching the news the whole ride back, different analysts suggesting this theory or that. They talk about what the world should do in response. Others tell us that we will never forget where we were at that moment. That this could reshape history. Some eulogies for employees working on the mining station play with sad music.

They cut to a message from Queen Olympia of Mars. She has ashen skin like most Martians and white wisps of hair, but she is still a young woman. She wears an elegant dress with gloves and sits on a simple stool, staring out a window at the endless crimson desert. The Martians aren't little green men. Their ancestors were people from Earth.

She maneuvers toward the camera in such a gracefully rehearsed form that it makes me sick. "As you have no doubt seen, the people of Mars have had no choice but to respond to Earth's continued theft of our natural resources." The Queen sounds regal yet robotic. Has she ever had a genuine conversation with another person? Hard to imagine based on my brief sample size. "Mars has declared war on Earth. We shall not stop until the pillaging of our resources has come to a halt." She stares out of the window again, all dramatic. "I hope that we can keep further casualties to a minimum."

Then the feed cuts off.

"Bitch," Val says, clenching both fists.

The world president held her own press conferences, declaring war in response. Denouncing the Martians. On and on. All mostly saying the same thing. We almost got home when Marcus broke his silence.

"You know what's weird? We didn't defend that station at all."

"What do you mean?" I ask.

"There were no androids to defend them there or anything. Just completely helpless. Like a fort on the frontier in the Wild West with no cannons or guns."

Val scrunches up her forehead as if surprised with herself to have missed this precious detail. "There's probably an explanation."

"Maybe," Marcus says.

When I get home, Emma and Aunt Gracie are on the couch watching the news. With tears, Emma jumps over the couch to hug me. She's gotten her hair cut short, just above her shoulders.

"Your hair's nice," I say.

She cups the bottom of her hair, giving it a little push-up. "Yours looks...terrible. What happened?"

I summarize the Monkoro tournament for her and how my hair got fried. It's one of those stories that usually draws interest but is overshadowed by current events. Everyone else seems upset, but I barely feel anything. I don't know anyone who was on that station. Bad stuff happens to people all the time. An all-out war with Mars is inevitable, but I won't be involved, and Earth will just send up an army of androids after them.

A fog has steadily grown in my mind over the day. I don't really, truly understand what's going on at all. I don't keep up with current events. My life is hard enough to worry about what problems the world has. Mars used to be a colony of Earth, but they declared independence a little after magic came out of nowhere. I felt too dumb to ask Val and Marcus any questions earlier.

"Why would they do this? I don't understand why they want to pick a fight like this or even stoop down to killing innocent people."

"You should pay more attention in school," Emma says.

"Yeah, I know. But I want to know now, though. Why do we hate each other? I just know that we do."

Emma smiles and looks smug. She's getting into her teacher mode. She loves it. Usually, I turn my brain off, but I'm genuinely interested this time. "When magic first started, society on Earth almost fell apart. You remember that, at least?"

"Of course, I'm not a total idiot." A billion young people wake up one day with the ability to shoot magical fireballs out of their hands. It was quite a mess. I can almost forgive the adults for strapping collars on all of them. Almost.

"It happened on Mars at the same time. Before, they'd send metals to Earth, and we'd send them back supplies they needed to live. The supply chain stopped while Earth reorganized, and by the time the world government replaced all the countries, many people on Mars died before figuring out how to survive without the stuff from Earth."

"I guess that makes sense, but it doesn't explain their hatred of us."

"The first time the new world government checked in with the people on Mars, they asked for an update on the metals shipment. Not, 'Hey, you guys okay? How are you doing?' Just asking for more stuff." Emma shakes her head. "Kinda heartless."

"Yeah, and the survivors left are all badass guys that aren't into taking that kinda crap, so they declare independence, and there's nothing much Earth can do about it."

"Badass *people*."

"Right, of course." I set myself up for that one.

"So tensions have been high ever since. Fighting over the asteroid belt has just set it right over the top. I could've understood destroying an unoccupied facility, but we had people on that one. The Martians are terrible, as far as I'm concerned. I hope our droids wipe them all out."

"Me too."

Emma goes to bed, and I stay up a bit with Aunt Gracie. "I just feel weird. I'm not as upset as everyone else," I say. "They're a bunch of people I don't know, and this was bound to happen sooner or later. More people die in accidents every day on Earth."

Aunt Gracie cradles a glass of wine in her hand. She gets exponentially more interesting to talk to the more she drinks. She sheds the outer layers of a 'full-grown adult' and becomes real. She smiles at me, letting me know she won't judge me. "Honestly, it's less grief for the people themselves. It's sadness for ourselves. That thin veil of security we once had is now torn to pieces." She takes a long sip.

"Security? We live next to a giant wall of water that could drown us all at any moment."

Aunt Gracie forces a laugh. "We have that. Now, Martians could drop out of the sky and blow us all up at any moment."

"I'm here to protect you," I say. What a dumb thing to say. What would I do?

"These people," Aunt Gracie pauses for a second, staring off into the distance, "these people are monsters. They kill each other and then use each other to fertilize the ground. Did you know that?"

"No. I didn't."

"They have more radiation up there, so they have more mutations. More babies with problems. They just take those babies and grind them up into fertilizer." She takes another long sip. "Monsters."

"Yeah, that sounds terrible."

The doorbell rings. Both Aunt Gracie and I bolt upright. Who could that be? The door camera reveals the hulking silhouette of a behemoth. It's Agent Charleston, with his sunglasses cover his eyes even at night. I think he isn't human. He might have android eyeballs under those shades.

I open the door to greet him. "Been a long day, Agent. Don't think I'm in the mood to scrap your bots right now."

Agent Charleston chuckles. "Nah, son. I'm afraid you'll be doing whatever I want. You belong to me now." He hands me a stack of papers.

"What?"

Effective immediately. You are a new defender of this beautiful blue ball of ours."

CHAPTER 9: 100% NOT JEALOUS

My bed's made and looks good for once. I never actually 'make' the bed. Why would I? I'm just going to sleep in it again less than 24 hours later, and my bedroom's not a display center in the middle of a store. It drives Emma crazy.

My suitcase remains empty and open on the bed. No need to pack clothes since the defense force will provide uniforms. Reviewing all of the stuff in the room, I can see that's all it is. Stuff. Some things manifest memories, happy and sad, while others just take up space. I have pictures of family and friends, but my phone has those. Posters of bands, a small shelf of books, and girls wearing as little as Aunt Gracie would deem allowable hang on the wall, but I'd feel weird bringing a suitcase of rolled-up posters.

After putting the suitcase away under the bed, I head back downstairs. Aunt Gracie and Emma sit on the couch while Agent Charleston stands with his arms crossed.

"Where's your bag?" Aunt Gracie asks.

"Don't need it."

Aunt Gracie raises an eyebrow. "Okay." She stands up and envelops me in her arms, and squeezes hard. I didn't need to power up for a pat on the back. My face gets red. I pat her on the back, the universal sign of, *okay, enough of a hug for now.* "Looks like you finally got what you wanted."

"What's that?" I manage to say despite my lack of air.

"Joining the military." She loosens her squeeze.

"I was thinking more of a normal branch. Not whatever weird racket this guy is in, but I'll take what I can get."

"Racket?" Charleston snarls at me, which is a look I have a feeling I'll be seeing a lot more of.

"I got three things out of this, though."

"Oh?" Aunt Gracie tilts her head.

"Military. No more working at the plant. And best of all, drum roll please," I hit my index fingers on an imaginary drum, "no more school."

"Is that true?" Aunt Grace asks.

"We give the recruits under eighteen a tutor. There's still school for them," Charleston says.

"Come on, seriously? We're fighting the first interplanetary war, and I will have homework?"

Charleston takes off his sunglasses to wipe them off on his jacket, revealing he does indeed have regular human eyes. He sighs. "Yes, the humanitarians will get all upset if we don't. You are technically children, after all. Teenagers with the force of an atomic bomb locked inside, but teenagers nonetheless."

I lean toward Aunt Gracie and whisper, "I'm going to skip class."

"Fine with me," Charleston says. He could hear that? Aunt Gracie just shakes her head.

Emma hugs me, too. "Don't let them change you too much, Jake."

"I'd like to see them try."

"Please, go ahead and change him a lot," Aunt Gracie says to the Agent with a grin.

"He has no choice in the matter," Charleston says.

"Ah, what would you need to change about me? I'm a perfect soldier already. I train hard. I want to win."

"You lack discipline and don't respond to authority."

"That's not true."

Agent Charleston puts his sunglasses back on. "You stole laughing gas from a dentist's office and then leaked it into your school's air conditioning."

That was *you*?" Emma gasps. Aunt Gracie holds her hands up to her mouth.

"Now wait, how'd you know that was me?" It didn't even work well. I needed to use *a lot* more of the stuff. Lesson learned. No, not to not do it, but to go big or not do it at all.

"The collars have GPS, Jake. Remember? You should keep that in mind before you go out committing crimes. I asked the police to hold off on you while I evaluated you. If you aren't on your best behavior, let's just say you're on track to join your mother."

"Wow, low blow there, big guy."

"It's Sir Big Guy to you."

Aunt Gracie and Emma say their last goodbyes and extra hugs for the road before Charleston and I head to the airport.

The lobby, mostly empty, is probably thirty freaking degrees. It may be a good idea to bring a jacket. I rub the sides of my arms. "Why do they keep it so cold in these places?"

"Just a big middle finger to the Earth," he says, which shocked me. I didn't think of him as an environmentalist type. We don't use carbon energy anymore, so that's irrelevant, but I'm not looking to pick a fight there right now. "Look, there's your friend. Go say bye. We're waiting on one more." He gestures toward the security line, where Marcus lugs a massive duffle bag.

"Marcus! What are you doing here? Where are you going?"

"North American Defense. I got drafted last night. Heading to Colorado."

N-A-D? That's awful. What's up with these defense force folks slapping together terrible acronyms?

"Hey," yells a familiar voice. Val appears and gives Marcus a quick hug. "Don't get killed on me."

"I never do," Marcus says. It's true. Unless it's Monkoro. Then he loses to little kids. I don't feel like reminding him right this second.

"What about me? Where's my hug?" I ask, waving my fingers towards me. "Saying goodbye to everyone, aren't you? Don't discriminate against the best-looking of us."

"Unfortunately, not," she says with a roll of her eyes.

"I drafted Val as well," Agent Charleston says.

"So, we'll be like squaddies together. Cool."

"She'll be captain of your squad," Charleston says.

Val smirks. "Yeah, so now when I give an order, like, to leave your collar on, then maybe you'll actually do it."

"Yes, of course, uh, Sir? Right, we're going with Sir?"

Val nods. Marcus gives us all a final wave off as he heads for his flight. We board our own small jet plane.

Tall buildings built on top of the old runways surround the airport. The planes can all take off vertically, so they don't need long stretches of asphalt to take off or land.

No other soul occupies the plane other than the three of us. Nobody else boards. No stewardess to give us a little safety demonstration. Not even a video. A computer pilots it. The plane lifts high above the city before twisting and accelerating towards our destination. My phone loses reception, so I can't tell what direction we're going, and the Sun isn't up, so I can't even use some of my old boy scouting skills…which I don't have anyway.

"Where are we going?" I ask the Agent. He laid down on a row of seats and had a pillow behind his head. Why hadn't I thought to ask sooner? I'm way too trusting of strangers. Amazingly, I've gotten this far in life, really.

"You'll see," he says.

I groan. "Do you know?" I ask Val.

She gives a little smile as if to say, *yes, but I'm in the mood to torture you right now.*

We fly over a vast swathe of darkness before a giant city sprouts up. I guessed it was Jacksonville, so we didn't go to the Gulf of Mexico. The plane flies east.

"Oh, Bermuda! Are we going to Bermuda?"

"No," Charleston groans.

"Somewhere in Europe, then?"

"No."

"Can you tell me what's going on?"

"Jake, shut up. I'm trying to sleep. I'll explain everything to you when we get there. I don't want to say it twice. Others are waiting for us. Get some rest. You're going to be tired." Agent Charleston rolls to his side and shortly afterward snores lightly in a way I'd expect a Disney princess to, not the giant over-muscled bull like the Agent.

I try my best to sleep but can't. Val props her head up against the wall with a pillow and closes her eyes. She barely breathes at all. She's kind of pretty when she isn't awake and feeding her metal fist into my face. I'll give her a 7 out of 10. I'm a 5 on the looks scale, but you throw in this personality, and then, POW, instant 8.

With the Sun coming up, the plane finally slows down, but there's no land in sight. The computer pilot doesn't communicate anything, of course.

Standing straight up, I can get an angle just below us. There's an aircraft carrier down there.

"A ship? In the middle of the ocean?" I ask.

"Where else would you put a ship?" Val laughs at her own joke. Have some class, Val. Leave the laughing at one's own jokes to me.

Charleston wakes up, makes odd gurgling noises, and puts his glasses back on. "We train you out here," he says with a yawn, "so you can't hurt anyone or destroy anything."

I imagine giant blasts of magic flying around and hitting buildings, cars, or animals and realize that that made sense, but couldn't we sink the ship, too?

The plane touches down with hardly a bounce, and we disembark. A few older crew members run around, but three people do not have uniforms. They're waiting for us, all about my age or a little older.

"Everyone, this is Val and Jake from North America," Agent Charleston introduces us.

The three of them nod. Then Charleston introduces them to us one by one.

"This is Raj from the British Isles. Say hi, Raj."

"Ello". He's disgustingly handsome with mahogany brown skin and jet-black hair. A manly five o'clock stubble covers his face and adds a rugged pinch to balance his proper accent. I hate him already.

"Raj averages at about a 900 level, but I once clocked him at 2,000, which is, quite frankly, terrifying," Charleston says.

Raj smirks. I hate him even more.

"This is Sun Li from Hong Kong. Say hello, Sun."

"Nǐ hǎo," Sun Li's petite and cute with short black hair. She has a stern face like she never smiled.

Agent Charleston puts a hand on her shoulder. "Now, interestingly enough, Sun Li's power doesn't show up on any detectors. We have no idea how strong she is right now, but based on some sparring, I'm guessing she's at about 1,000." Sun Li nods politely as if that number means nothing to her.

"Finally, we have Igor, from—"

"Russia!" Igor raises his arms into a flex as if he had just won a wrestling bout. He doesn't wear a shirt but has some odd fur pelt wrapped around him. A bear's face sits on his shoulder with the fangs permanently embedded into his ski.

"You seem to be wearing your, uh, cousin," I say.

"I fight bear. I wear bear."

"Are you saying that you're a werebear? Like a werewolf?"

"No, I wear bear."

"Yeah, you just said that."

Agent Charleston cuts in, "Igor's English is not so great, but I'm hoping that will improve through this experience."

"What about us? Going to introduce Val and me?"

"Oh, that." Charleston walks over to me but points at her. "That's your captain, Val. This is Jake, definitely not your captain," Charleston says. "He clocks in at, on a good day, around 500." The others laugh, and my smile dissipates. "The reason he's here is because of this chart."

The Agent withdraws a tablet. It has a graph with a sharp spike that then goes back down. "This is Jake's output at a power plant on his first day. Topped out at 5,000."

That number makes everyone serious. "That means Jake, for one second, was by far the most powerful person on the planet." Charleston folds up the paper and puts it away. "I'm lucky I got a hold of you before the Magilectric Department did. After I heard about what happened in Orlando for the Monkoro games, I had to scoop you up before someone else. Now, part of what we'll do here is improve ourselves and try to help Jake grow his power and be more consistent about it." He glances at his watch. "Oh, I almost forgot. I believe you all have met X-53 and Z-94." He hits a button, and two lockers next to the small building on the ship open. Out walk the two androids.

"Hello," X-53 says. "Good to see you all again.

"I'M GONNA RIP OFF YOUR ARMS." Z-94's face is still cracked.

"Ha! I like heem," Igor says.

"I thought we destroyed those things," I say.

"I remember Val doing that. I remember you running away." Charleston smiles. "Their memories and personalities are loaded onto a network. The 'cloud,' if you will." He makes air quotes. "We can just load them back up into a different body. It's part of an experiment with artificial intelligence. We're hoping they get smarter as they fight people more. We call their model the Phoenix."

"Sir, may I ask, why are we here?" Raj asks. "The Space Force is sending thousands of bots to lay siege to Mars. I don't see much point in a manned operation, but there must be some reason."

"Someone who respects authority and knows the right way to ask a question. Unlike some others I know." Charleston lifts up his sunglasses, and his eyes pierce through me.

I've had about enough of Raj already. Suck up.

"I'm glad you asked, Raj." Charleston takes off his sunglasses completely and draws in a deep breath. "Now, let me tell you everything that I know."

CHAPTER 10: WHEN PIGS FLY

Inside the ship, the hallways have huge tubes painted red and yellow, like veins bringing blood all over a giant creature. I almost stop and yell, "What are these for?" but continue as nobody else seems as curious as me. We reach a small conference room with a screen to project images on. The rest of us grab a seat. "This is a lot like a classroom," I say.

"What's the matter? Allergic? Remember what I said about continuing your education? This is more what I had in mind," Agent Charleston says with a wink. We connected there for a moment. Something must be wrong.

Turning on the projector, the Agent loads up a little presentation. "Raj asked an excellent question before. Why are we here? Now beyond the existential bull crap, we're here because this war with Mars is about to get very real and very close to home."

"How? It would take them around nine months to get here." I blurt out. See, I know stuff.

Agent Charleston glares at me for a second, then continues. "Six months ago, a few vessels left Mars on a trajectory for Earth." In the presentation, some blips of dots on a solar system map leave Mars with a dotted line showing its trajectory.

"Now, this isn't enough for an invasion force," Charleston says. "A few dozen, we guess. Queen Olympia sends people to Earth without permission all the time, so this isn't anything new. Diplomats. Athletes for events.

Performers. Anything. They'll ask permission a few days before because they know Earth won't say no at that point."

Sun Li raises her hand. "Sir? Do we believe this is a small attack force to engage in guerilla tactics?"

"Or, hey, why not bear tactics?" I'm dropping jokes here because this is getting too serious.

"Yes! Bears!" Igor lifts his arms up in a flex.

Val puts her hands to her face. Agent Charleston groans. "Yes, that's what most of the defense force community believes, but most aren't worried about it. Many regions just sent almost all their armies into space to invade Mars."

"Sir, if I may?" The disgustingly handsome Raj breaks in. "Why would they do that knowing that Martian troops could be three months out?"

"A show of force. Politicians are under a lot of pressure to respond to things immediately. Sometimes, without much thought as to the long-term consequences. It's a decision some will surely regret." He switches off the projector. "But that's where you all come in. Now, some regions have the resources and population to train their own makeshift defense force. But there's a slew of places out there that won't have anyone to defend them, and that's what we're here for."

"Do we know how strong they are?" I'm contributing now in a serious matter.

"Their soldiers are about as strong as ours. No real difference there, according to some peaceful sparring we've done with them in the past. Many are tough enough to tear apart dozens of our bots alone."

"Do they wear collars like we do?" Sun-Li asks.

"No."

"Are we getting ours taken off?" I touch mine. It's feeling awfully tight right now.

The Agent sighs. "No."

A few gasps erupt in the room, not from me. Nothing surprises me. Ever. Really. Still, I have to point out how dumb this is. "But we've got people coming here ready to invade. You'd have us fight them with one hand tied behind our backs while they pummel us with two?"

"It's not up to me. People are afraid of what you may do without your collars on."

"Sir, but you've taken collars off during evaluations," Val points out. It's my first time seeing her take my side in anything.

"Yes. Removing one or two collars for evaluations or games of Monkoro is one thing. Opening up all the cages in the zoo is another."

"So that's what we are? Just animals?" I ask.

Charleston grins. "Sure. He's a bear. These guys are lions. Not sure what you are. I'm thinking a pig."

"Funny."

"Here's the part that you will like, Jake." Agent Charleston heads toward the door. "With your companions wearing collars, you won't be so far behind."

"I think we're going to be best friends, Agent."

"I thought we already were. Now, everybody outside, let's get started."

My stomach grumbles. "Sir? Food?" I don't carry a mocking tone that time. Food is a serious business.

"Right, I forgot you're humans, but I've got to go. Val, get them some grub, and then get your training started. I'll be back in a week or two to see your progress. No magic blasts till I get back. Melee only. Try to get to the point where you can fly with your collars on."

We eat breakfast in the ship's cafeteria. My school's cafeteria is similar except this one doesn't have windows and the food tastes worse. Why do I hate school again? Everything else seems just as bad or worse.

Sun Li sits across from me, which is nice because she hasn't talked or laughed at any of the crap about me yet. Val and Raj sit at another table far away. They talk, Val with an enormous smile on her face. Raj does his best job of flirting with her. I grip my silverware tightly. Igor, the werebear, eats his food while standing up. He scarfs it down in 20 seconds.

"Is it true that you can't even fly yet?" Raj asks me from his spot a few tables down.

"Yeah," I reply with a mouthful. "So what?"

Raj shakes his head. "I don't see how you'll be helpful in just a few months. We'll have to protect you the whole time, mate."

"You heard what Charleston said." Then, I make air quotes. "'Most powerful person on Earth.'"

"For a second, mate. Could've been a screw-up with the measurements."

I give him a big smile, making sure to have as much food in front of my teeth as possible. "We'll see in a minute," I mutter through the mouthful.

We clean our plates and head outside. I feel exhausted for the morning. It's like I hadn't slept and flew on a plane all night. Oh, right, that *is* what happened.

"Okay," Val says, starting us off. We circle around her along with the droids, Z-94 and X-53. "Let's pair up for some sparring. Igor, you face off against Z. Probably a good idea to keep the two psychos together."

"I WILL DESTROY YOUR GLUTEAL CLEFT," Z-94 pounds its chest.

Igor laughs. "Das good. You remind me of my father."

"Sun Li and I will spar over here. Raj and Jake, you guys face off down that away. Keep some space."

The ship's deck stretches farther than a soccer field, and we leave plenty of space between groups.

"I'm ready to see how you'll protect me, knight in shining armor," I say.

"As long as it all ends with me getting a kiss from the fair maiden," Raj replies, glancing at Val.

"It ends with my foot in your ass, Raj."

Charging at him, I don't give either of us time to power up or concentrate. We exchange punches and kicks back and forth, most getting blocked, but some landing.

I connect one roundhouse to his ribs, and Raj grunts, exhaling everything in his chest, but then he lands a fist right into my cheek, sending me flailing backward and onto the ground.

"Alright, switch partners," yells Val. With my face on the ship's deck, I move my jaw around to ensure it's still attached to my face.

"Good round, mate. Let me give you a hand," Raj says from behind me.

I turn over and reach up as if to accept his help, but then flip my palm to him. Charging up as much magic as I could in a split second, I unleash a blast into his chest, and then he flies backward before falling back down like a rag doll.

Val runs over to him like a concerned mother, holding his head up. "What the hell, Jake? No magic. And the round was over."

"He was being an asshole."

"No, Jake. You are the asshole. You were always the asshole. Now get out of my sight. Go to your bunk. Z-94, bring him down there and make sure he doesn't screw anything else up."

Performing my best tough guy walk, Z pushes me to the ship's control tower entrance. I glance at Raj, and he gives me a little wink as Val helps him up. I flip him a middle finger while she's not looking.

Z-94 leads me below deck to a little room with the thinnest mattress I'd ever seen.

"So, looks like I got sent to my room without dessert."

"I'M ABOUT TO BASH IN YOUR FACE 'TILL YOUR TEETH FALL OUT!"

"Oh God, please don't yell, we're inside." My ears ring. Z-94's bearable outdoors, but in here, the sound bounces around until eardrums rupture.

"Just leave me, I'll be a good boy."

"THIS IS MY ONLY VOLUME."

I plop down on the thin mattress as Z-94 waddles away. Every spring in this thing swirls up and pokes my body. As tired as I am, I don't think I could ever sleep on it. After my ' time out, ' Val eventually calls me back,' and we train some more.

Things are like that for a few days until I'm up early one morning, standing on the edge of the deck and watching the sunrise. The others started to fly while sparring, and I'm always stuck on the deck. I have to fight Z-94 or X-53 because the others already surpassed me.

The breathtaking view fascinates me, though. We're on top of essentially a tall building overlooking the water. I startle myself with how high up we were. It's the kind of fall that could kill you since the water would be like cement once you gained enough velocity.

"How's your mental status?" Val's snuck up on me. She admires the sunset, too.

"Good, never better," I lie.

"I can tell you're frustrated."

"Nah, I'm fine, really."

"Sure, your tough guy acts as transparent as glass and just as fragile."

"Uh, bullet-proof glass. With a real dark tint."

"Yeah, okay. I just want to let you know that your power is still increasing. Just because you can't levitate yet doesn't mean the training's not working."

"I just can't get the hang of it."

"The rest of us learned to fly with collars off. You have to do it differently. Don't compare yourself to us. It's a different situation. We'll just have to try new techniques with you."

"That's...actually kind of reassuring. Thanks, Val. It's almost like you think I'm a real person."

"No, you're still just a bad impersonation of one. I'm just captaining."

I flick her metal arm. *Ting*! "So, trained without a collar on. That's the most I've learned about you yet."

"At first, sure."

"Help me out here. Don't make me fish for info. Your mysterious girl routine is getting as old as, uh, an unrefrigerated sandwich."

"That's the best you got?"

"With mayo on it. It's growing moldy fuzz everywhere."

"Nice."

"Please?"

Ah, the magic word, surely she can't deny...

"Project Valkyrie. That's where my name comes from."

"What's that, a TV show? Your parents are kind of weird."

"You're as dumb as you look." She scuffles up my hair. "Oh yeah, Agent Charleston's coming back tomorrow."

" I'm not even flying yet. Can you ask him to wait?"

"Nope. You're just going to have to learn. Today."

"How?"

"Remember? New techniques," she says and shoves me off the top of the ship.

CHAPTER 11: DOGS

Falling headfirst off the ship and hitting the water might kill me. Rather than try an acrobatic flip, I power up quickly and tighten my fists. My collar vibrates as it jolts me with everything it has.

The water comes closer and closer. I raise my arms in an X above my head, screaming as I gather up as much energy as I can into my arms. My eyes close just before impact.

But nothing happens.

The surface of the ocean indents in a semi-sphere, as if a giant glass bowl presses down into it, but not far enough for the sides to fill in with water. Little bubbles form around it, and steam rises at the edges.

Val peers over the edge of the ship at me. "That's it! Now, fly back up here."

I grit my teeth and try my best to gain control. It feels like floating underwater, except the water boils, and my skin's like flames dance all around it. A ring of fire is around my neck from the collar. I manage to 'push' the feeling of weightlessness down from the center of my body towards my feet. I rise higher up into the air, still upside down.

Once I reach the level of the ship's deck, Val says, "That's about as awkward of flying as I've ever seen. Try to spin yourself around and land on your feet."

Maneuvering myself, swinging my feet down underneath me, I spin slowly right-side up in the air, magical power still flowing all around me. Finally, my feet touch the ground.

Val smiles. "I think you kind of overdid it with the power. It doesn't take *that* much energy."

I grunt and throw a lazy punch at Val. She quickly dodges and knees me in the rib cage, doubling me over. Then she backhands me in the face with her metal arm, sending me tumbling down the deck of the ship.

My magical energy dissipates along with most of my fury. Val stands above me with a cocky grin. "You still wind up too much with your punches when you're mad. You'll have to work on that. You don't always need to land a haymaker."

I want to say, "Screw you," but I can't since there's never going to be air in my chest again.

Charleston shows up the next day, just in time, and watches us sparring with each other in the air above the ship. He nods with approval and then lines us up on the deck. "You all have made great progress. Now, I've got you some presents."

He rolls a crate on wheels out of the plane and opens up the top. We rise on our tiptoes to try and get a peek from where we stood at attention. Agent Charleston reaches in and pulls out a breastplate made of flexible plastic, but a layer of red cloth in a mesh pattern adorns the surface.

"These are for you," Charleston says. "This material will protect you from heat, while the mesh cloth here is a bunch of inflatable cushions. Like a life vest. If you get submerged in water, then you'll float up."

"Why we need that?" Igor asks. "We fly. Like birds." Were-bear-birds? This is getting out of hand.

"Because now you'll fight over the water with all-out magic blasts. Two of you will always protect the ships from any magic that misses its target. Otherwise, you shouldn't worry about hitting anything. We're not in any trade lanes for shipping. The inflatables will make sure you don't drown or at least give the others a chance to rescue you."

"So, when we train, we should go all out?" I ask.

Charleston nods, then tosses each one of us a breastplate. "Go on, put them on. I need to know if they fit."

It's tight on me. I need to get used to how the compression fit around the chest, but at least it didn't restrict breathing. It just feels like latex. Uh, don't ask how I know what that feels like. The front of the piece has big pecs and sculpted abs like we were superheroes or something. I give it two big thumbs up.

"Alright, now get to it. I'll be back in a month."

"A month?" Val asks. Everyone else calculates how long it takes until the Martians show up after that point. I'm not bothering with the math. They can tell me.

"Yeah, I've got things to do. I trust you won't play spin the bottle or games on your phone the whole time."

"Our phones don't work out here," I say.

"Yes, that's by design, actually. Oh, and I have bad news. Your tutor is coming in tomorrow." We all groan in response. The Agent gives us all a wave as he headed toward the plane. "So long. See you in a month. Now, get to work."

We practice hard after that. Ten hours a day. Raj is the only one who regularly visits the tutor. We sometimes have to take a day or two off after getting hit by a particularly powerful blast head-on. Val decides if we're faking it, but most of the time, she lets us determine whether we are okay to spar again.

The powers between us are relatively even. We differ in the little techniques we develop. Sun Li can send magic down her whole arm and lash it out ahead of her like a whip instead of just blasting it out of her palms. Raj bends beams of his magic midflight, whereas most of us could only shoot in straight lines. Igor opens his mouth and lets loose intense magic blasts like some of the androids. X-53 and Z-94, neither individually as strong as any of us, can work together by putting their arms together and weaving magical beams that strike simultaneously. Val's ability to use telekinesis through her metal arm is the most useful. She can control magic beams midflight, sending them away or turning them right back at you if you aren't careful.

The rest of us can copy Val's power. If we store energy in a hand or fist, we can slap or punch magic beams in another direction. It takes a lot of practice because if you hit a blast head-on, it just explodes in your face instead of getting deflected away.

Raj and I have brutal fights. We'd both need rescuing after bouts. Once, Val flies over and picks Raj out of the water, giving him CPR. Another time, I dodge one of his blasts, just barely, and while I mock him, he spins it back around and hits me in the back. I wake up to Igor pumping my chest and breathing into my mouth.

I groan. "Saved by a werebear."

"No! I wear bear," Igor roars.

It makes me laugh every time, even on the brink of death.

One night, I can't sleep. This shouldn't be surprising because, for one thing, I'm never surprised. Remember, old cereal boxes glued together must make up my mattress. I saunter up to the deck of the ship. It's pitch black, and I can't see a thing. There aren't any lights at all. Usually, something like this would have a blinking red light on the tower so it doesn't crash into something else in the dark. Being a secret is more important than safety for this group.

There's a full moon, though, and a tiny speck of a torso and head on the ship's side. Somebody's out enjoying the night's sea breeze.

"Don't jump! You have so much left to live for!" I shout.

"Suicide's not funny," Sun Li calls back.

It's not easy being a joker, I tell you what. I sit beside her, and our feet dangle over the edge.

"What're you doing out here?"

"The stars. Just looking," she says.

"Know the constellations? Over there's the Big Dipper. My favorite is Orion. Easy to spot with the belt right there." My last memory of my Dad is him showing me patterns in the stars and their names and the difference between stars and planets in the sky. Stars twinkle. Planets don't. That's the simple version.

"The Chinese made their own constellations. Like this one." She traces a pattern in the sky. "They're smaller than the West's."

"That's cool. I never knew about that."

"Yes. Quite interesting that two different peoples can look at the same thing, come up with different ideas, and neither of them is wrong."

"It's one of those nights where you're going to get all profound on me, huh."

Sun Li smiles and tucks some of her black hair behind her ear. "My mother always said I was a deep well full of water."

"What do your parents do?"

"Not much. They're dead."

"Oh." This is awkward. Traversing a dead-parents conversation. I don't want to say the wrong thing, but I can't say anything at all. "How?" I manage to ask.

"They were magilectric engineers. Died in an accident." At least she's opening up to me, unlike Val, who (whom? I never can remember; I also really don't care) I still know nothing about.

"No parents. Well, we have that in common. Dad's dead. Mom's in prison."

"We may not have family, but at least we have each other." She pats me on the back. "Good night, Jake." She gets up and heads back inside.

"G'night." Did I just make a friend? Cool.

♧

After about a month, we line up on deck as Agent Charleston lands and re-evaluates us. "I loved these numbers you sent me, Val. You're all improving nicely. I have a tough time believing that Jake's gotten his power up that much, though."

"Why not?" I grin. Then, throwing in a "Sir" after a short delay. "Do you want a demonstration, or will you just leave again?"

"Sure, let's see what you've got," Charleston says.

"All right, who do you want me to go up against?"

"Me," the Agent says. He removes his tie, unbuttons the top of his shirt, and takes off his jacket, throwing it to the ground.

I laugh. "You? You're old. I didn't even think you had any power."

"I know it's the worst kept secret on the planet, but if you don't work in the plants, your magic doesn't get tapped out. I still have some energy left in my tank. You'll see."

"I don't want to hurt you or something. Besides, you're not wearing a vest."

"Don't worry about me. Worry about you." Charleston smiles. "Let's go."

We fly above the ocean at each other, exchanging blows. I don't use magic blasts as it becomes clear how much more powerful I am than the

Agent. He can barely keep up. Eventually, he waves his arms in the air, and we both land back on the ship.

"That was a lot of fun," he says between breaths. "I think you're all ready to become DOGs."

"Sir, what does that mean?" Sun Li asks.

Charleston brings us to a room with a chair and a tattoo gun on the wall controlled by a computer. He pulls up his sleeve to reveal his mark of the snarling dog again.

"Now, you don't have to get the symbol on you. But you also won't get into the best parts of hell if you die without it," he says with a smile.

We each get the tattoo one by one, and the rest of us bark as the tattoo gun finishes each one. It's the first time I feel any sense of camaraderie between us. It's as if we're a real team made to defend the Earth rather than just a bunch of people blasting each other with magic out in the ocean.

Charleston doesn't leave this time. He stays with us and trains, claiming that he'd wrap up all his business and that the rest must take care of itself.

One morning, about two weeks before the Martians are scheduled to arrive, we all sit in the cafeteria eating breakfast. We joke and reminisce about battles we'd fought against one another, poking fun at our own blunders, congratulating each other's progress. Raj even smiles at one of my dumb jokes. While I still have this awful feeling in the pit of my stomach whenever he and Val met eyes, I can control it now. I don't lash out anymore.

Just as we finish breakfast, Agent Charleston opens the door, slamming it against the wall. His giant body takes up the entire door frame.

I'm startled and manage to fumble some words out. "Sir, I know it's my turn to clean the bathroom, but I just didn't get around to it last night. I swear I'll do it right after our first session," I say.

"Shut it, Jake. They're here."

"Who's here?" I ask.

"The damn Martians."

CHAPTER 12: AGE OF DECEPTION

Charleston briefs us inside the ship. Every face in the room is solemn. I don't even crack a joke, which shows incredible willpower on my part.

"Sir, how could they land weeks in advance without us knowing?" Raj asks.

"They must've sped up somehow." The Agent turns on the projector. "We don't have sensors all over the solar system. Just a few, mostly around Earth and Mars. Fewer around Mars now that they're actively destroying them."

About a hundred dotted lines of assorted colors race across the screen around Earth, each ending in clusters around the globe. "They left their craft outside of our defenses and then flew down at these locations." The lines end evenly around the planet but with a dozen in Russia.

"My homeland in trouble," Igor says.

"I agree. Even though they can defend themselves, it'd be a good idea if you and someone else went there," Charleston says.

"I take Jake. He and I make great-big-grand team." I have no idea what would make the Werebear think we worked well together.

Charleston thinks that over for a second. "Okay. Sun Li, you take X and Z over to Brazil. Raj and Val, you guys head over to South Africa." Great, more quality time between Raj and Val. I'm over it, though. It doesn't bother me. At all. Really.

"How are we going to get there?" I ask. "We only have one plane."

Val puts a hand on my shoulder. "You can fly, can't you?"

"I've never flown internationally before. Jake Airlines. I like the sound of that." Humor chip reactivated. That restraint lasted, uh, two minutes.

"Also got you guys some new hardware." Charleston brings in a box smaller than the crate that held our armor. He reaches in and pulls out a collar.

"You got new leashes for your dogs?" I ask.

Charleston glares at me. "These have better GPS and radio communications. Press this button to talk back. They will work as long as we don't lose the satellite network." Charleston puts the new collars on us and then removes the old ones. "They also have a little less bite than you're used to. You can power up more before they start to shock you. I had to pull a lot of strings for that." He sounds like a used-car salesman.

With my new collar on, I concentrate some magic into a fist, and a blue aura formed around it. The collar doesn't hurt me at all with that low of a level.

"What're we waiting for? Let's send these dust bunnies back to Mars," Val says.

We march out onto the deck of the aircraft carrier and stand on the edge in a row, powering up with magical flames licking all around us. "You lead the way," I say to Igor.

"That would be wise," he says, in a tone and accent I hadn't heard before. I expected him to say something more like, *you follow me, little cub.*

Raj and Val blast off to the southeast while Sun Li and the bots go southwest. Igor leads the way to the northeast for a trip across the globe. We don't talk the entire way. For one, Igor's not a great conversationalist, and the wind whipping around the ears while in flight makes it hard to hear. Charleston gives orders and corrects flight paths for the other two groups, but Igor seems to know the way to go, accounting for the Coriolis Effect and wind for a long-distance flight. I may have underestimated the Werebear.

We can't fly as high as an airplane because the oxygen gets less concentrated the higher up we go. For all our technology, we don't have anything to warn us other than feeling woozy. Passing out and falling to death isn't ideal, but staying below the cloud line is a safe bet.

Over oceans, fields, hills, rusty cities, rivers, and highways. The air grows colder, and I get more and more bored. The inflight entertainment includes the magnificent views, but sad to say, those grew old after a while.

Igor descends and leads me to the center of an abandoned city. Concrete featureless buildings line the streets. No cars. No people. "Wait here. I have to run errand."

"What the hell are you talking about? Gotta' go pick up some milk at the store?"

Igor grins. "Yes. Some milk. For my bear cub." Then, a magical fire glows around his body, and he blasts off into the sky, abandoning me in a serial killer's paradise.

Shattered glass covers the streets. Broken children's toys are scattered about dilapidated apartments. Armless mannequins line up in-store displays, frozen in a conversation that no one would ever want to hear. Creepy.

I press the radio transmission button on my collar. "Hey, Charleston. Igor left me in a scene from a horror movie. Can you tell me where I am?" A minute passes and hit the button again. "Val. Raj. Stop making out and let me know if this thing works."

Nobody answers.

"Government-issued garbage." I puff out my chest and stood in a stance like Charleston would. "Pulled a lot of strings for this." Mocking the Agent feels pretty good. I should do it more often.

Two guys emerge from behind a corner down the street. "Oh good, humans. Hey!" They might not speak English, but I also don't speak Russian or whatever language. I still don't know where I am. Eastern Europe,? "American. Uh, Yankee!" I yell.

Their footsteps grow louder and echo off the concrete buildings as they slowly stroll my way. They have similar haircuts, the sides of their head buzzed but long hair on top, swooping over to cover one side. Each has the hair parted to the opposite side of the other. Each has the same face, twins. Mirror images. Their clothes cling to their thin frames and have an odd fashion. Their pale skin has never been touched by light this close to the sun. Necks are absent of collars. Martians.

"Thanks for saving me some time searching for you, I guess." I press the radio button and whisper, "Igor, where are you?"

The twins walk toward me like they have all day to pick a fight. Maybe they do. I hold my ground but feel a strong urge to power up and fly away.

"Relax." A hand rests on my shoulder. A girl a bit taller than me with long black hair and thick lips frozen in a permanent pout stands behind me. "We are not here to fight you." How's she able to sneak up behind me? Martian ninjas? The world is screwed.

"Oh really? You came all the way here to play hide-and-seek with me in Eastern Europe." The twins loom right behind me now. The weird thing is, even though I could fly up, I feel trapped with people on either side of me.

"For you? We're here to talk. There will be time for fighting later. You'll see. Follow me." Black spandex pants rest low on her hips, and her top is cut short to reveal a belly with soft curves outlining her abs. She walks away, and her butt moves in unison with her swaying hips.

"It's not very genteel to stare," says one of the twins as they pass me.

"I wasn't. I was, uh, following."

"Sure."

The tall beauty leads me to an alleyway and pointed to a door. A sign with a man having a liquid poured over his head hangs next to the entrance. I can't read the language. "I assume this is a bar and not a waterboarding clinic."

"Go, funny guy. Just go." She doesn't follow me inside.

A dozen candles light the inside. Broken glass and bottles cover the floor. A man stands behind the bar, pours a drink, raises it in my direction, and says, "To friends and freedom." He flings the glass back so fast that I'm not sure he has to swallow. He's got a receding hairline with a crop top and a giant bald spot. A leather jacket with a few tears in it covers his torso.

"I thought you would've toasted to war and the death of innocent people," I say.

"Nah. Too many words." Thin strands of hair attempt to cover the top of his scalp. Huge bags hang under his eyes. He must've been drinking for days. He holds up the bottle. "They don't make it this good on Mars. Let me tell you."

I sat down at the bar like any old patron might as he pours me a glass. I'm old enough. But why would he care? I try my best to down the spirit, but the back of my throat's boiling about halfway through. I gag and slam the glass down.

"What'd I tell you? That's some serious swill."

That was stupid to drink that. It could've been poisoned. Don't be stupid, Jake—it's time to get serious. "I'm outnumbered here. Say what you want to say to me, and I'll be on my way."

"We're going to have a chat. That's all. I want to feel you out. See what you're about." He brings a candle closer to us. A scar races diagonally across his face, and his right earlobe has a giant chunk missing like it'd been a snack for a rabid raccoon. He's like an alley cat on the last of its nine lives.

"The name is Regolith. Rego to anyone that's not my mother." He extends a hand.

"Jake." I don't shake.

He puts his hand back down to his side. "Yes, I know who you are and all about you." He fills himself another glass to the brim. "You want that collar off, and I know you think it's bullshit that anyone has to wear it at all."

"Sure, so what?"

"Did you know that we don't wear collars on Mars?"

"Yeah."

"We don't have giant walls of water to hold back—just a little atmosphere to keep in. Everyone volunteers a little bit of their power to keep society together. They aren't forced to with bribes and a lack of other options."

"What's your point here exactly?" I try drinking the rest of my glass. It's as pleasant as sipping gasoline, but I do start to feel, well, excellent, like the connections between my joints are looser.

"What will you get if Earth wins this war?" He leans forward, shadows dancing across his face in the candlelight.

That's a great question. I don't have to think about that very long. "Nothing. I get nothing."

Rego picks up his glass and tips it toward me like he's awarding me a point on a game show. "Exactly." He downs another glass. "Now, with us. You'd have freedom. Your people would have freedom. We'd slowly pull down the ocean walls, leaving up only the places necessary for farming to keep everyone fed. How's that sound?"

I can't lie, that sounds good. Too good. "You're trying to manipulate me."

"Yes. I am. But not for some nefarious reason. I want to win, and I think you can help us do that. I also believe that you want us to do that." He pours another glass. "Oh, did I mention that your mother wouldn't be in prison anymore if we won? How silly of me."

"Listen. That all sounds great. I can't deny that. I don't like how all the people my age are involuntarily enslaved, but I can't take the side that kills innocent people."

"Oh, that little thing. Here's the kicker of this whole pitch I'm giving you." Rego downs his drink and then leans close like he has to tell me a secret: "That wasn't us. We didn't do it."

CHAPTER 13: UNLEASHED

It's not every day that a Martian lies to your face. "Sure, you didn't blow it up. It just did that all on its own." I swirl the little bit of booze in my glass and then throw it to the back of my mouth. It doesn't go down right. My body shivers, and my face cringes with disgust.

"You're telling me Earth had these cameras conveniently placed around the station just in case we attacked? With perfect shots of teddy bears and baby booties floating through space?" Rego rocks his head back and forces a laugh.

The worst part about this conspiracy theory is that it makes too much sense. "But why would they want to go to war with Mars?"

"Hell, if I know." Rego walks around the bar and sits on the stool next to me. "Probably resources. The asteroid belt. Maybe they see this as an unavoidable conflict and would rather start now while they think they have the upper hand. Wouldn't be the first time in history." He takes small sips of his drink now. His words start to slur a bit.

"Why would I take the side that starts their invasion by getting plastered? This is crazy. I'm leaving now."

"Ha. Invasion. We were invited for some sparring. We turned into an invasion after Earth blew up its own mining station." Rego stares at the wall and scratches his bald spot. "And I'm drinking because, in the next few days, I'm going to do things that would horrify a normal person. Likely things I may not be able to live with myself afterward."

"What about the video of Queen Olympia taking full credit for the attack? She didn't say it wasn't you guys. Why would she do that?"

"We *were* in a cold war. The Queen's looking for any reason to get things going."

"Whatever, Martian Man. I'm out of here." I crush the glass in my hand, the shards not even piercing my skin, and walk towards the door.

"Okay, okay, you're gonna make me do it. Break out the big information. I wanted to keep this a secret a while longer, but you leave me no choice."

I stop and look over my shoulder. "What is it?"

"Your collar. It's a bomb."

"No, it's not. Get out of here."

Rego laughs. "I can prove it, too. Follow me." He stumbles, trying to get off his stool, and leads me outside. He shields his face from the sun with a hairy hand like a vampire emerging from its den. "I think you've met Helliana." He points to the attractive girl. She leans against the wall across the street.

"The twins are Phobos and Deimos, after the moons of Mars. I can never remember which is which. Don't think it matters. They'll answer to either name. Right, morons?" The twins sit at a broken cafe table. They glance over and give a little wave. "See? Now, let's get our little Russian spy over here." Rego puts his hands over his mouth like a megaphone. "Igor, come on out. Your cover's blown."

Igor emerges from around a street corner. "Surprised, Jake?" A smooth, calm accent has replaced the weird bear vibe he had going. This shouldn't surprise me, seeing as Igor led me straight here and abandoned me. Rego rushes inside the bar and comes out with an interesting tool. Something might be used for trimming a bush, but the handles are metal instead of rubber to draw magical power. "We've been jamming your collars since you got close. That's why your radio doesn't work. But if the collars are removed wrong...boom!" Rego makes an explosion with his hands. "Your head's a watermelon."

Rego puts the blades around Igor's collar. "Ready?"

"Ready."

Rego powers up a bit, a thin haze of magic building up around his arms. I'm still not used to seeing older people use magic. He tenses his muscles as he tries to cut Igor's collar off. Rego twists the clippers from side to side and opens and closes the blades a few times, veins popping out of his biceps until the collar falls to the brick pavement with a clang. Rego picks up the collar and holds it up for me to examine. "Now, as soon as this goes outside our jamming radius. It's going to blow up." His arm cocks back like a baseball pitcher, but he throws the collar straight into the air.

Light flashes, and a small mushroom cloud blooms up into the sky. "A freaking mini nuke? They have a nuclear bomb in our damn collars?"

"You bet. They can't have their dogs go unleashed without the ability to put them down," Rego says.

I can't believe they would even consider the option. They are some combination of Agent Charleston and the United governments. Everyone and everything in power subjugates us. "I have to go."

"I was afraid you'd say that. You're going to do something stupid like confront them about it just to make sure it's true." Rego reaches into his pocket and pulls out a disc about the size of my palm. "You still don't believe us? At least take the jammer with you. That way, they won't pop your head like an atomic pimple when you call them out."

Shoving the disc into my pocket, I'm unsure who or what to believe. Without another word, I blast off into the sky and toward the aircraft carrier.

How could Charleston, no, the world, stoop this low? The clouds rip apart as I fly through them, probably higher than I should. Don't care. It's a long trip back, and I have a lot to think about. It *could* be possible the Martians lied to me. Maybe they switched out Igor's collar. Rigged it to explode. But who am I kidding? These are the same people who have no problem stealing our magic. Our energy. My fists clench, and I power up, flying close to the ocean to shred apart the surface, leaving behind an extended wake.

The fact that it's even possible that I'd risk my life for them with a bomb strapped to my neck. A bomb that they put there. They drain us dry until we become a part of them. And we're the ones that die in their wars. Well, you know what:

Screw them.

I slam onto the deck of the ship. The deck dents in and cracks all around. Crewmembers scramble away, and an alarm blares. "Get Charleston. Get his ass out here now!"

Magical flames rise all around me. My collar flares at my neck. I barely feel it.

Charleston stumbles out the door, not dressed in his suit and without his trademarked sunglasses. He's weak. A lot less mysterious. I can crush him without even thinking about it.

"Jake. You're alive. You went off the grid. We thought you were gone."

"You strapped bombs to our necks!"

Charleston, startled, trips back toward the door. "How?" mutters out of his lips before he realizes that he just incriminated himself.

"So, it is true."

"I had to, Jake. It was the only way they'd let me give you collars that would let you power up higher."

"And the station? That wasn't even the Martians, was it? It was them."

He scrunches his face. "Them? Who? You can't be serious. You're letting the Martians get into your head right now. Of course, Earth didn't destroy its own station. All those innocent people. No. Just no."

"I don't believe you. You're probably too low on the totem pole to know anyway." Charleston doesn't answer me. His silence says it all.

"I'm done wearing this." I grab the collar with a hand on either side of my neck and start pulling. Magic swirls all around, and the collar shocks my neck. It feels like a colony of fire ants fighting a war around my neck and fingers.

"Jake, what are you doing?"

Magic flames spin around me in a tornado, and the ship groans under our feet.

"Jake, stop. You're going to break the ship apart. You'll make the collar explode."

That just pisses me off even more. I shift my hands so that it will break at the opening. I don't even care if it blows up. "You're lucky I don't just kill you right now."

I scream, collecting as much power as I can. My collar goes into overdrive, glowing hot, burning my skin with temperature and electricity.

The magnetic latch of the collar finally snaps. A magical font of energy pours out of me like nothing I'd ever seen or felt. It's like a volcano had built up intense magma for millions of years and finally unleashed its maelstrom of fury.

A shock wave pulses away from me, slamming Charleston into a door. A series of ominous cracks echo out from the ship. The bow and the stern fold in as the carrier sank from the center.

The ship's crew pour out the doorways wearing lifejackets and prepping lifeboats. Charleston pushes himself up onto his elbows. His back might be broken. "Jake! You're going to kill these people."

I throw my collar off the ship as far as I can. When it gets out of the range of the Martian jammer, it explodes, leaving behind a small mushroom cloud. It's the final validation of truth I need. I can't feel any guilt from what I do from here on out.

It's war, dude.

"You killed them. Not me." Magical flames surround me, and I shoot off into the sky. Smoke billows out from the ship, and there isn't a sign of rescue for miles. Should I help them? Nah, they'd get onto rafts. They'd send out an SOS. They will be okay.

As I fly back to the Martians, it's clear I'd become what they feared most. I'd become exactly why they forced the collars on us in the first place, but the only reason I chose this path is because of their fear, because of their imprisonment.

Who are *they?* Some collection of old people. Politicians making decisions to imprison young people like me. Officials elected by 'citizens' that could vote. The irony is that I can't even vote yet, but they take and take and take. Strap bombs to my neck. I can't support that sort of society any longer.

I rip through the air and landed in the abandoned city. The glass in the remaining windows of the nearby buildings shatter and fall to the cracked concrete below. Rego, Helliana, and the twins all wait outside. I land in the middle of the street and toss Rego his jammer.

"I assume this means you're with us now," Rego says.

I nod.

"Good." He lifts an eyebrow at me. "How'd you convince them to take your collar off?"

"I tore it off."

Rego laughs. "That a boy! Remind me to look for you the next time I can't open a jar." Everyone gives him a confused look. "I'm kidding. That's never actually happened. I can always open jars…"

"Sure, old timer." Helliana winks.

"What next?" asks one of the twins.

"The other squads are taking out android factories all over," Rego says. "But we haven't made any strikes against the big boys. With our new scarred-up friend here, I think we can start."

I touch the rough, bumpy skin on my neck. Through my phone's front camera, I see the ring of scarring where the collar had been. While I'd removed the metal one, this is a collar I'd wear for the rest of my life. I'm not fond of turtlenecks, either.

"But first, I need to tell you something." Rego points at me.

"What?"

"I need to tell you the goal of this war. The real goal."

"Isn't it just to control the mining of the asteroid belt?"

"Nah. That's just a reason. Really, we're here to take over the Earth."

None of that made any sense. "Rego, Mars doesn't have enough people to rule over Earth. That's just crazy."

"Jake. If we don't win. Then both our planets are screwed."

CHAPTER 14: JUPITER

Rego's talking gibberish. He's red-faced and clearly, the booze has destroyed his brain.

"What are you talking about?" I ask.

"Helliana, give it to him," Rego says.

She walks towards me with long, muscular legs. To say she was out of my league doesn't capture her. She's out of my universe.

"Yeah." I raise an eyebrow. "Give it to me." I restrain a laugh.

She slams her palm into my forehead, and her fingernails dig into my scalp.

"Not what I had in mind."

Black blurry discs pop into my vision until darkness surrounds me. A blue orb and a smaller red one spin around each other. A man made of lightning coalesces between them, extending out giant hands and crushing them both, crumbling the spheres into dust.

It all fades away. Then the orbs return, dancing around each other, but this time, the red one lands on top of the blue one and cracks it. The man of lightning appears but can't fit his hands around the two conjoined spheres. Then he slips away into the darkness.

Reality returns with Helliana still digging into my scalp.

"Uh, thank you for that," I say.

"Did you see it?" she asks.

"Oh yeah, I saw something all right."

She releases my head, but it still hurts like a baseball player had just hit a home run off my forehead. Her nails had nearly drawn blood. How did she insert images in my mind? "The vision. What did you make of it?" she asks.

"God plays weird marbles? Or we should put away our glassware before the giant space monster breaks it.

Rego rubs his head. "Ugh. I will need more to drink if this is the best we can steal from Earth. Listen, you don't have to get it. Or even care about it. As long as you're on our side."

"If your goal is to free us and take off our collars, then I'm on your side."

"Good." Rego taps a couple of buttons on his armband. A hologram of the globe hovers above it with circles, and the letter X scatters across every continent. "Here are the targets we've hit and the targets we need to. Mostly bot production facilities. Some others are research centers for magilectric weaponry. The ones we know about anyway."

I study the maps for a minute. "You're missing a lot of places. There's a big factory just south of Tallahassee that I know about. They just make parts there, not the whole droid. Actually, there aren't any targets near the coasts on here."

Rego nods. "We figure they'd be more heavily guarded, so we leave them for later."

Makes sense to me. "Where do we start?"

"You and Helliana can head here." He points to a spot way north of where I'm from, somewhere in the Appalachian Mountains. "They have a factory there that makes droid batteries. Military grade. Me and the twins have business elsewhere."

"Limited casualties, right?"

"I care about the buildings. If they can't make parts for droids, then we win. It's not like the people on this planet know how to fight. Except for a few. Let them live if you want."

"Of course, I want them to live."

"Your choice. You've got a long trip ahead of you, so get started. Helliana, make sure he doesn't fall asleep and dive into the ocean. He's logged in a lot of miles already today."

"I will, and if we do a decent job, maybe I'll give him a present." Helliana lightly scrapes a fingernail across my cheek. I'm not sure what present she's talking about, but I'm pretty sure that I want to open it.

Helliana launches herself into the sky. "Come on, follow me." She goes straight up, and I trail behind her. We cruise for about an hour over land and sea before something rumbles in the clouds above us. Vibrations dance deep within my chest. Whatever it is, it's big.

I spin around to face the clouds, flying with my back to the ocean far below. The clouds part and a giant bot the size of an airplane swooped down. "Holy crap!"

Extending a hand, I power up a blast. Helliana pushes my arm just as I let the charge go, sending it off into the clouds.

"Jake, stop! That's with us."

"What the hell is it?"

It has a giant robotic frame, human-shaped, but with plates all around its chest. Cracks and crevices between the plates glow with red. The powerful magilectric battery inside of it gives me goosebumps. Its deep vibrations conjure waves of nausea inside of me.

Jake Airlines doesn't come with a barf bag.

"Its name is Jupiter." Helliana flips around again to face forward. I head alongside her to try and talk, though it is tricky with the wind ripping by our ears. We have to scream at each other.

"I thought Mars was behind with magilectric technology."

Helliana winks. "It's complicated."

Jupiter has a cavity in its chest with a glass dome over it. That could be a cannon. This is the first time I've seen something like it. So huge. So powerful. The droids Earth has don't compare.

"How many more of these are there?"

"Jupiter's the only one I know of, but I don't know everything, Jake. I'm just me."

We cruise until land creeps over the horizon. Helliana points up. The two of us and the giant robot angle upwards until we soar far above the cloud line. She brings me close to Jupiter's torso and retrieves two hoses with masks attached from a compartment in its chest. We strap them on over our faces, and I breathe deeply, finally getting the oxygen I need to be this far off the ground.

"Incoming ballistics," Jupiter announces in a deep, gargling robotic voice.

Three missiles swoop toward us, fluffy white clouds forming behind them like a trail behind a jet plane.

I rip off my mask and fly away from the others. One of the missiles follows my path. Pre-magic age weapons don't work well because their targets can blast them out of the sky now. I lob a fireball toward the rocket and sped away, expecting it to explode.

Nothing happens. The missile has somehow dodged it with compressed air jets, my fireball trailing off into the distance. I shoot another, and a burst of air comes out of the side of the rocket. That nudges it out of the way just enough.

Fireballs wouldn't work. I charge up a beam and fire while tracking the rocket. It dips and dodges away before I finally connect right on its tip. The explosion and shockwave part the clouds.

Jupiter, flying backward, powers up a red beam. It should take care of its own missile. Not gonna' worry about the giant robot.

Helliana speeds forward but the rocket has almost reached her feet. "Crap," I say before launching myself in its direction and pushing against the side of the missile. It veers away from her. I pump my fist. Saved the day again. Then, the rocket unleashes a loud beep. "Uh, double crap. That can't be good."

It's warm. Then hot. Then I fall. I fall a long way. Something catches me, and my senses return while I lie on the dirt, head resting in Helliana's lap and Jupiter towering over us.

"That was close." One of my hands crunches some dead leaves on the ground as I regain my movement. Trees surround us. The setting sun's light filters through the branches, and the glow dances on Helliana's face.

"You saved me." Helliana strokes a hand through my hair. "I owe you one."

"Can I open that present now?" I try to smile. Not sure my face works yet.

"No, but I'll let you touch the wrapping." She leans down and kisses me; a fire spreads from my lips and stomach, then through my whole body. As hot as the missile made me feel on the outside, she makes me feel on the inside.

I leap up from the ground. "I feel better."

Burn marks cover my clothes. The DOG logo on my chest has peeled off as it hangs like an opened banana peel from my chest plate. My sleeve has torn completely and exposed my DOG tattoo. Forgot about that thing. Could I melt it off with magic? Might hurt. Would need some of Rego's booze to take the edge off. The really screwed up thing is if I could survive a missile blast, what would it take to kill me? Worse, finding out means coming dangerously close to dying.

"How far are we from the target?" I ask.

Helliana points at an opening in the trees. "There." A factory surrounded by the forest sits at the bottom of a hill with clouds of smog pumping out of its smokestack. "We can blast it from here, though there might be more of it underground," she says.

"No. I have to make sure all of the people get out."

"We can't wait. They know we're here. We have to hurry."

"We're not going to just blow up innocent people. If that's what you guys are about, then...then."

"Then what? There's not another side for you to join, Jake."

"I'll make my own side."

We fly to the factory, and then I tell her and Jupiter to wait for me outside. Pausing at the door, I take a moment to dwell on the awesomeness of the moment. Me barking orders at Martian lady and a giant robot. Then I bust through the entrance.

Dozens of workers in blue uniforms stand along a conveyor belt. Long robotic arms attach pieces, but the workers do the others. A sign on the wall says, "Days Since Last Accident: 320". Afraid I'm about to take off the first two digits. I conjure up a small fireball and throw it up into the ceiling. Bang! Everyone spins around. I have their attention. "Time to leave people, let's go. Evacuate."

They don't need to be told twice. The workers scramble toward the exits. I grab a lady with a tie on, assuming she was the manager. "Make sure everyone is out of here." She nods, her hard hat falling forward and covering her face for a second.

She flips on the fire alarm, but I still follow her through the building and downstairs through the basement as we comb through each room to ensure everyone left.

After everyone left the building, most of the cars in the parking lot disappeared, too. "Go. Get out of here," I say to the manager, who fled toward the last vehicle.

"That took too long, Jake. We can't do that every time," Helliana says.

"Afraid I have to."

Something roars through the air. Sounds like fighter jets.

"Too late, they're here." Helliana's hands turn to fists, and she scans the sky.

Jupiter's head completely spins around on its body. "Targets acquired. Awaiting orders."

Three soldiers land near us. Clouds of dust blow away, and leaves scatter at their impacts. They wear blue jumpsuits with the Earth's Air Force symbol, an image of the planet with a giant plane flying around it, on their chests. Collars are strapped to their necks.

The one in front is tall and a big black puff of hair. It's Marcus.

And he's pissed.

CHAPTER 15: JAKE'S FAVORITE CHAPTER

Marcus touches a button on his collar with a radio built into it. "Got 'em," he says.

Both groups stare each other down. "You got any questions for me?" I ask.

"Nope." Marcus doesn't move. His face has no expressions. No anger. No surprise. Is he actually a droid? That wouldn't shock me.

"Really? Not even like a," I spoke in a deeper voice, mocking Marcus. "'Jake, what are you doing siding with the Reds?' Or, 'Jake, how's it going, buddy? I missed you.'"

"Nah."

"They strapped bombs to our necks. They don't care about us. You have to understand."

"Don't care." He rubs the collar on his neck. "Gonna' kick your butt. Then on to the next one."

"It won't be like before. I've gotten a lot stronger over the last few months."

"Me too."

"I'm not wearing a collar. It wouldn't be a fair fight. Why don't you guys leave here and let me do what I must do."

"Nah. You ready?"

"Let's do this old school—you and me. The loser's side leaves. That way, I spare your two friends, and then you don't force me to use my giant robot."

"Okay."

I smirk, tuck my elbows in tight, flex all my muscles, and gather my energy. Bolts of lightning swirl around me. Without my collar, the power comes so much faster now and—

Marcus bolts right at me, so fast I can hardly see him, and slams an elbow into my face. The blow shoots me thirty feet back into a tree. Thud. Prickly splinters scratch my back. All the air leaves my chest, and I struggle to suck any back in.

The old Marcus would've let me power up all the way. "Ugh, come on. What happened to sportsmanship?" This isn't the old Marcus. He's a soldier now.

I push myself off the tree, leaving behind a depression and cracks in the trunk. Marcus speeds toward me again. His fist misses my face after I duck from the blow.

We exchange punches, blocking and kicking each other. He powers up as we fight, something I haven't learned to do. He grits his teeth, roars, and punches at my face. I catch the blow in my hand, but it's so powerful that my fist slams into my own mouth.

Blood seeps from my lips and nose. I wipe it away with my forearm like a little kid with a cold. How can he still be this strong? This fast?

Marcus barges at me again. Relentless. I pant and gasp for air while he's not winded at all. His fists are everywhere. He hits my chest. Ribs. Cheek. He lands a flat palm to my ear, and a thousand church bells ring in my head.

A brief opening in his defense appears, and I connect a blow to his chin, sending him off into the distance. Now's my chance. Gathering my energy, I scream as the bolts of energy flowed around me. A shock wave surges from my body, and the surrounding trees uproot and fall.

The sun sets into a glorious red and orange glow over the hills. The darkness won't affect this fight. Both Marcus and I glow with furious magical energy.

He shoots out from the dense brush while holding a cocked fist behind him, ready to launch a fierce blow. I dodge just before his punch landed on a tree. It explodes into a puff of bark and sawdust.

We jump off trees, each one falling after every leap, colliding with each other into a torrent of punches and kicks. I block as many as possible while he shields himself from most of mine.

Both of us land on the ground ten yards apart. The entire hillside's been stripped of its trees. Our fight has brought nature, at least in this valley, to its knees.

"Not bad, Jake."

"I'm just getting started." I dart toward him, but he falls backward. He plants a foot into my chest and uses my momentum to fling me into the air.

Marcus launches after me, kicking into my stomach, which sends me even higher, then flies behind me and unleashes a powerful beam into my back that sends me plummeting back toward the ground. A cloud of dirt puffs up into the air like a dynamite explosion funneling out of a mine shaft.

When the dust and smoke clears, half of my face is buried. I flip over and can't open the one eye caked with dirt. Upturned trees and logs smolder around me as I lie at the bottom of a crater caused by Marcus's attack.

He lands next to me and glares. "Surrender."

"I feel pretty beat. Good match."

"If you don't surrender, then I have to kill you."

"Okay. Okay." I hold up a hand. "I—"

A red beam, as tall as Marcus and big around as a truck, slams into him and sends him careening off into the side of the crater, pinning him there before it explodes.

Jupiter charges another round out of the canon in its chest but aims it toward the factory. Helliana assaults the two other soldiers so they can't interfere with Jupiter.

I struggle to stand and then limp over to Marcus. His giant puff of hair has burnt away along with his eyebrows. "You alive?"

He groans.

"Sorry, man. This isn't how I wanted this to go."

"Go...away."

The factory walls lie in chunks. I float up to Jupiter and grab onto his leg. "Helliana! Let's get out of here." The giant robot flies upward, and she chases after it. The two soldiers shoot magical blasts at us, but we dodge each one. We get so high up that we use the oxygen masks from Jupiter while the two soldiers have to retreat.

Helliana and I crawl into a small compartment inside of Jupiter that's warm, but we still wear our oxygen masks. We tried sleeping. She lies with her butt pushing against my crotch, and that makes it very difficult for me to drift off. But I have no energy left at all.

Rego and the twins are inside the candle-lit bar with the sign of the stick figure getting liquid poured over his head.

"How'd it go?" Rego asks. A half-full glass sits on the table in front of him. Wafts of smoke dance in the air as a cigar rested between his cracked lips.

"Done." I stretch my neck from side to side.

"Good." Rego taps the monitor on his arm and brings up the hologram of the Earth. The circle that symbolizes the plant morphed into an X. "Ready for your next mission?"

"Come on. We just got back. Mission successful. Can't we celebrate?"

Rego laughs. "I like you already." He stands up, reached behind the bar, and lifted a bottle with clear liquid inside. "Vodka. Straight from the motherland. Too bad Igor's not here." He lines up six little glasses and fills them up to the top.

There's me, Helliana, Rego, Phobos, Deimos, and... "Who's the last one for? Can't you Martians count?"

"The Queen, you dumb Earthling. You'll learn. We're going to toast." We each grab a glass and raise them into the air. Rego holds up two. "To Queen Olympia, long may she live. And to stolen friends." He smashes the drink for the Queen on the ground. Everyone cheers and then drinks.

And another one. Okay, lots more drinks.

We sit around the table with glasses in hand. "Tell me about Mars. I don't know much about it." The only things I've learned about the red planet came from TV and movies. It has a few oceans now, but you still can't breathe the air there. Everyone lives in cities under bubbles made like Earth's ocean levees.

"You're gonna' love it." Rego leans back in his chair and puts his feet on the table.

"I'm going to love it? What do you mean?"

"I mean, you're going to go there someday, stupid. On our glorious home world, nobody works in plants all day. Everyone has magic. Sure, it depletes as you use it, but they're not stealing it from you like they do here."

"Fighting tournaments," Phobos says.

"All the time," Deimos says.

"Really?" If there was one thing I enjoy in life, it's fighting. Flying around, unleashing magical blasts. Nothing feels better.

"And Queen Olympia? She's amazing. Wisest woman in the universe. I'll introduce you to her." Rego reveals his hideous yellow smile.

"You mean, you've met her? Know her personally?" I have never met anyone important. Not even the mayor of Tallahassee.

"Everyone meets the Queen. Everybody! When you're seven years old, you must climb Mount Olympus to meet her." Rego keeps up his smile like he's living in the past.

Helliana raises an eyebrow. "Some die on the way up."

Rego waves his hand, dismissing it. "Ah, it's just a rite of passage. Not that many kids die."

"Other stuff you wouldn't be used to, " Phobos says. He whips his hair around so it's on the same side as his brother's. To be honest. I don't know which is which. "The highest power level you achieve determines how many kids you can have."

"That's bizarre. So how many kids could I have?"

"Probably around three. It's hard to tell. I haven't clocked you lately without your collar on. Hell, I haven't even seen you fight in person yet. Something I'll have to check on." He chucks his vodka to the back of his throat and pours himself another glass. "We have some arranged marriages, too. Usually between two powerful people so they can have the most kids possible."

Thinking about marriages gets me started on girls. I wonder what Val would do the next time she saw me. Probably rip my guts out. She already has.

Helliana sits next to me. Sober, she's ten out of ten. I was sitting at that table with vodka in my veins and swimming in a miasma of happiness. She's a goddess.

"Hey, can I open that present now?" I ask, mainly as a joke but half seriously, too.

"Yes, great idea." She grabs my hand and led me upstairs.

The next day, I stomp down the stairs with a slight headache. Rego's right where I left him. "There he is. How'd it go, champ?" I'm starting to warm up to him. He's not quite a dad figure, maybe like a drunk uncle.

"Pretty good," I say, trying to play it cool, but my cheeks started to warm. Helliana comes down the stairs behind me.

"First time?" Rego slams his cup on the table, demanding an answer.

"Nope."

"It was. Definitely." Helliana smirks.

Now my cheeks are on fire. I change the conversation. "What's the next target?"

"You're off to China with Phobos and Deimos. Haven't had much luck in that area."

"Can't I go with Helliana?" I ask for obvious reasons.

"Nope. Unfortunately, you two are a thing now, so I can't send you on missions together. You might sacrifice the mission for your partner."

I hold up my arms and gesture towards the twins. "But you'll send those two together."

Rego stares off into space as if this is the first time he'd ever thought about it. "I don't think they have souls. I'm not worried about it. Anyway, you'll see for yourself." He holds up his glass and sips as if cheering his decisions.

"Alright," I say, accepting his orders. It's something I've never done well. "What is it we're doing in China? Another android facility?"

"No. You're going to hunt a ghost.

CHAPTER 16: GHOST

"Rego. I think you finally drank too much." I take the glass from the table. "A ghost?"

Rego leans back his chair and puts his hands on his stomach in a strange, satisfied pose. "The ghost killed two of our people. I sent three after a research facility in the mountains in Asia. Only one came back. She was talking crazy stuff about a phantom. I think they must have some cloaking prototype given to one of their soldiers."

"So, we take out this ghost and then the research facility?"

"If you can find it, yeah. That's the plan."

"What about Jupiter?"

"Jupiter's been out fighting the good fight all night while we've been here being humans." Rego grabs his drink back from out of my hand. "I tell you what, those Earth military guys had that in mind when they all tried to transition to mostly droid armies. All work and no play make Jupiter a productive freaking war machine."

"When do we go?"

"Right now, if we could, but I understand you all have to sober up probably. Can't properly hold your liquor, you kids." He points to the back. "Coffee or tea back there. Eat some of our rations. Then get going."

After devouring a few mouthfuls of dried potatoes that taste like paper, I've got to let them know they live like barbarians. "This tastes awful."

"You're supposed to add water and heat it. Turns it into mashed potatoes, dummy." Rego shakes his head. "Don't they teach you anything on Earth?"

"We don't have a microwave. How do you heat it?"

"You're a walking fission reactor. Time to open up your mind, little dude." Rego piles some of the powder onto a metal plate, adds water, and then holds his hand underneath until it steams. He stirs it with a fork, and the dish slowly congeals into something almost edible.

"Ah, I get it now."

"Before you go. Take this." Rego throws me an armband. "You'll need it TO be able to navigate the globe without having to rely on everybody else like the little freeloaders you are." He winks.

"Thanks." I strap it on. It has a monitor that wraps around the wrist. Buttons everywhere. I'll have to play with it on the way.

"You can use it to scan for power levels. The ghost doesn't show up on it, but you should be able to pick up on anybody else. Even droids. So, you ready?"

"Yep."

"Good. Get on out of here. Find some warm clothes because it's way up in the mountains. We haven't found the facility, so you'll have to search around."

I scrounge up a nice jacket and some gloves, another layer for socks just in case. I have no idea how cold it would be. I'm from Tallahassee. What do you wear when it's freezing? I don't know. I've never seen snow.

Nothing bothers us the whole trip. No missiles. No androids. We must've had a significant effect on Earth's defenses already. It's stupid of them to send almost all their droids to Mars in retaliation, and I bet the leaders realize it by now. I haven't seen the news, but I can st imagine them barking at each other, wondering whether they should try to bring the androids back or not.

We soar for hours and finally land on the side of a snow-covered mountain. It's not as tall as, say, Everest, so we don't need to wear oxygen masks from Jupiter (who's not even here).

Dark grey clouds hang in the sky like a vast quilted blanket. Snow floats down like something out of a movie, and when the wind flurries, it flakes upward as if gravity meant nothing. I'm at the center of my own snow globe. Magical.

"Isn't this amazing? Have you guys ever seen snow before? Does it snow on Mars? Maybe it does all the time.

"No." Phobos holds a hand out to catch a snowflake with no emotions on his face.

"To what? The amazing part or seeing snow part?"

"Both." Deimos scrunches his nose as he stares at the sky, disgusted with the whole thing.

"Did you all have to split a soul when you were in the womb or something?"

"Soul? We gave that to our brother," Phobos says.

"Brother? You guys were triplets?"

"Yes. He failed the climb to Mount Olympus summit," Deimos says.

"Weakling. Maybe it was the soul weighing him down?" Phobos grins, showing a mouthful of unusually sharp teeth.

I shiver, but not from the cold.

We canvass the mountains while searching for the research facility or anything, really. Cars. Smoke. Ventilation shafts. Instead, there's just snow, rocks, and trees. A white rabbit scampers away, a white blur on a canvas of white. If my cousin Emma were here, we would spend the rest of the time searching for it. *Aw cute*, she'd say, and we'd try to lure it out of its little hole. I wonder what she'd think about me switching sides. I hope she'll understand in the end.

"Must've been bad intelligence on the location of this place." Phobos lifts a boulder to glimpse underneath. Had it come to that? I'm not desperate enough to check under every freaking boulder.

"I don't see any signs of roads or anything." I scan the mountains again. Even if snow covers the roads, there must be some sign of their construction, right? Could they have flown everything in by helicopter?

"This is stupid. Let's go back." Deimos searches under another boulder twenty times his size. I'm in the mood for being awed, I suppose. The things that magic allows for us to do. "It's not a person that's a ghost. It's this entire facility we're searching for."

As the words stumble out of his mouth, the ground rumbles. A huge hole opens in the valley below, and thousands of droids emerge like a swarm of bees. They rise as high as the mountains' peaks and levitate in a sphere's formation.

We crouch down and hide behind some rocks while keeping an eye on the massive airborne army.

"Can we take them?" Phobos asks.

I laugh. "Depends on the models. Maybe a couple dozen. Maybe a hundred if they're weaker, but that many? They'll grab us by the limbs and tear us apart. Better hope they don't see us."

The cloud of droids hums in the air for a while before splitting off as if they all received their orders. They burst into different directions, probably headed to all corners of Asia to defend themselves from the mini-Martian invasion.

"Okay, let's go in," I say.

"Let's just blow off the top of a mountain and cover the place with rocks," Phobos says.

"No, there might be people in there."

Phobos rolls his eyes. "Waste of time."

We skid down the snow and into the hole in the valley floor. It opens into a massive warehouse with columns stretching from the floor to the ceiling. A few droids stand in circles on the ground while hundreds of other empty circles form a pattern on the floor. "Maybe they're broken." One has a model name in Chinese. A language that I am about as familiar with as ancient Sanskrit. It's basically an awesome dragon language written from sharp talons into stone. I wish I had taken the class in school.

These droids are a lot like the Western ones except for the attention paid to ornate designs on the metal plates, and they have more colorful designs. The Western models are made for war, but an artist designed these. It'd be a shame to blow them up. Even their eyes, rather than just one dark lens like sunglasses, simulate a real person's eyes. Kind of creepy, but kind of cool.

Out of nowhere, its freaking head explodes like a glass cup falling to the ground. A shard of it whizzes past my head, and I narrowly dodge it. It would've been buried in my eye had I not moved.

Phobos outstretches his hand; magical energy crackled between his fingers. I breathe in to yell at him, but the other dozen androids hop into fighting stances.

"About time." Phobos launches himself at one, exchanging punches and kicks, before two more come to help. Phobos dances between the three droids.

Deimos fights six by himself. The droids grab his arms and legs, and he punches and kicks them away, but he'd get overwhelmed soon if we didn't do something.

I force energy from the core of my body out into my fists until blue auras flow around them. A droid charges at me, but I punch at its chest. It tries to block, but my blow shatters its arms and goes straight through its torso. It powers down and then crumples to the ground.

Droids launch at me as I try to get closer to Deimos to help. I knock them away, shattering them into the nearby walls and columns. I've almost reach him when a stick of crimson emerges from his stomach and then disappears. His mouth falls open, and he reaches for the wound. Something moves behind Deimos, and the air distorts just a little bit when it moves.

"Ghost!" I yell. I grab Deimos and fly him to where the opening in the ceiling. "Phobos, get over here."

Phobos kicks off a droid and speeds over. He glances at Deimos but doesn't say a word.

The droids surround us.

"Get the columns." I hit a column with a fireball and then the next, over and over. Phobos does the same. Soon, the ceiling collapses, crushing the droids, and a mess of metal with snow surrounds us.

"Did we get it?" Phobos asks.

"I'm not sure." If the Ghost moves quickly enough, I'd see the air distortion. He will probably tiptoe toward us, but we might hear its footsteps in the snow. "Just stay quiet and listen."

The wind whistles through the debris, and Deimos gurgles through his bloody mouth. "I'm sorry, guy, we'll help you in a second. Put some pressure on the wound. Both sides if you can." Hmm, he might not actually be able to do that right now. Need to do something different. "Phobos, try to cauterize his wounds while I listen for the Ghost."

"Nah, he's dead. No point." Phobos scans the rubble instead.

"What the hell's the matter with you? That's your brother!" I kneel beside Deimos. His eyes are wide. The Martians all seem fearless until death stares them in the face. I concentrate energy into three fingers, making them hot with magic. My power scorches and singed, and small black puffs of smoke rise from Deimos' stomach and back.

He screams in agony before passing out.

The bleeding stops. "That's the best I can do."

Nothing moves around us. "Maybe we got him trapped under there," Phobos says.

The rubble quakes as the Ghost bursts out from underneath, sending snow and debris flying everywhere. He wears a gas mask, and the stealth machine kicks back in as invisibility rolls over him, starting at his feet, rising to his head, and then going back down.

The sword slashes in wide arcs as the Ghost tries to keep Phobos and me away. We can't get in close enough, but we duck out before the Ghost could hack at us.

I power up a beam and fire, but the Ghost holds the sword's edge out in front, cutting my beam in two and sending it blasting into the rubble.

Ghost holds his sword up and gathers energy in the other hand. Then he throws a magical whip around Phobos's neck. I've only seen one other person use magic like that. Phobos grabs at it but doesn't make a sound as the magical loop squeezes his windpipe. Ghost pulls him closer to finish him off with the sword.

"Phobos, fire!" I launch a magical blast at Ghost and then dart to the side, firing another. Phobos unleashes a powerful beam out of both of his hands.

Our masked enemy can't dodge them all. He lets the magical whip dissipate and tries to block, escape, and slash at all our attacks but fails. The explosions fling him into the rubble.

The stealth technology stops working, and Ghost comes entirely into view. The clothes have been burnt and torn in certain places. The missing sleeve reveals a DOG tattoo on his arm. It's the same tattoo that I have.

CHAPTER 17: SHOWDOWN

I kneel next to the Ghost. Many people must've trained as part of Agent Charleston's defense group. It couldn't be someone I know. I peel the gas mask off his face.

It's Sun Li. Her eyes are shut, unconscious, and her hair matted from sweat despite the current temperature.

"Know her?" Phobos asks. He picks up the sword and examined it.

"Yeah. She's a friend. Let's bring her back. As a prisoner." I walk away from Sun Li to check on Deimos, who is still breathing.

Shing!

I spin around. Phobos had stuck the sword right in the middle of her chest.

"What the hell's the matter with you? Why'd you do that?"

"No prisoners." Phobos wipes the blood off on her shirt.

"That doesn't make any sense. We're trying to free everyone from the collars, remember? Free the planet? They are prisoners."

"She was a soldier. Not a prisoner. Now, let's go. I'm cold." Phobos levitates off the ground, sword in hand.

"Are you going to get your brother?"

"Nope." A haze of magic surrounds him before he flies off, probably back to Rego.

These Martians are just animals. Sun Li's wound bleeds profusely. I try to stop her bleeding as much as I can, but it's a wound all the way through.

Her breathing slows and slows and slows. "I'm so sorry it came to this." At least she's dying in her sleep. I remember when we sat on the ship together during our training. What was it she said? It felt profound at the time.

I still feel nothing. This pit in my chest is more guilt for not feeling sadness or sorrow. It's more my conscious saying, "Hey, you should feel bad," when I don't.

What's wrong with me?

I lift the barely living Deimos off the ground and head back to the headquarters. It's another long trip back. What just a few days before had me in awe is now dull. I need music or a book to read. Something. Anything. But a lot can go wrong if you don't pay attention to where you're flying. Like ending up in a jet engine turbine. Minced into ground beef in midair.

The problem with the dangerous concoction of time and boredom is the second-guessing of every decision you've ever made. Would Sun-Li have spared me if the roles were reversed? I don't know. I want to think she would have, but she's a soldier, too, and I was her enemy.

We land in the abandoned city with Rego and Helliana standing outside to greet us.

"Ghost got Deimos. Doesn't look very good," I say. Deimos is still breathing, but he had not moved the whole flight on Jake Airlines.

Rego studies the hole in Deimos's stomach and wrinkles his nose. "Damn shame. Well, put him in a bed upstairs. We'll do what we can for him."

"We got the Ghost, though. She had this sword." Phobos holds out the sword to Rego, who takes it. "We broke the cloaking device, but I brought it just in case we could reverse engineer it."

"Great news. Good jobs, boys. And the sword works? It doesn't break?" Rego asks.

"It did this to Deimos," I say.

"Good point."

"Can't we bring Deimos to a hospital? Maybe Russia or something? Don't you guys have allies?"

"No. Can't trust 'em. Can't trust anybody. We'll do what we can, Jake."

I haul Deimos upstairs. We celebrate that night again. Apparently, the whole operation's shutting down factories, magilectric weapons research facilities, and droid storage warehouses all over the planet.

"At this rate," Rego pours everyone another drink as we sit around a table, "the Earthlings might overthrow their own government for not surrendering to us." He makes an extra glass and holds two glasses above his head. "To Queen Olympia."

"To Queen Olympia," everyone recites.

"And to lost friends," I say.

"Deimos is not dead yet, friend." wasn't referring to him. Rego smashes one glass on the ground and slurps on the other one, and the rest of us join him in the toast. My alcohol tolerance was low before I joined up with these guys, but at this rate, I wouldn't even get a buzz from a whole bottle.

I take a sip. "I still have questions about this whole war."

Rego holds up a finger. "Let me use my predictive powers. The answers are as follows: Yes. No. And finally, I have never seen a gorilla, let alone one riding a unicycle."

"I don't think those were answers to my questions."

"Oh, weird. Must've been an alternate universe or timeline." He waves a hand in the air. "But seriously, what inquiries are running amok in that little brain of yours."

"We're destroying these facilities. Then what? When will they surrender?"

"The wonderful thing about fighting a loose alliance is that they will fall apart. Some parts of this planet will surrender soon." Rego holds up two hands parallel to each other. One tipped over and hit the other one. "Dominoes. They'll all give up."

"I don't see it happening. They do have that wave of droids heading toward Mars after all."

"Yeah, we'll have to take care of those to crush their hopes. I'm not worried about it. You've seen what we can do. Imagine a whole planet of us. Those droids aren't going to scratch the surface."

"Then what?" I ask.

"Geez, such an inquisitive little strategist today."

"I'm just trying to figure out what the plan is."

Rego swirls his drink in his hand. "If they don't surrender after their attack fails, then we launch a counterattack. Given the work we've done here, they won't have a large defense force. This war is over in eighteen months or so. That's the plan."

"How do we free everyone from the collars without flooding the world? What's the plan for that?"

Helliana places a hand on mine, her fingernails lightly scratching my skin as her hand comes down. "Let's worry about that *after* we win. Okay?"

Her warmth spreads from my hand, up my arm, and through the rest of me. I relax. Smile. "Fine. All right. How about you tell me about yourselves? I hardly know you for a bunch of people I'm willing to die with."

"To die for?" Rego ask.

"I'm willing to die for freedom and the freedom of others. That's why I'm here."

Rego grins, a chorus of yellow teeth unveiled by his thin lips. "Here's us. Phobos is a genuine psychopath. But you knew that already. It's why I love him. I'm a grunt. Born and bred military man. Helliana here is interesting. Or should I say Duchess Helliana?"

She rolls her eyes. "Please don't."

I nudge her. "Ah, come on, Duchess. You gotta explain that."

She removes her hand from mine to gesticulate through her tale. "On Mars, each city has a Duchess. It's sort of like a mayor or a governor on Earth. My mother's the Duchess of Valhalla."

"The best damn city in the solar system." Rego holds up his glass.

"You're the next in line to rule a city?" I ask.

"Basically. Mom's still going strong, though." She holds up a hand and made a fist. "I'll have to fight my sister. I know I can beat her for it. She's more into books than fighting."

"You fight to the death or what?"

"Sometimes. Or the other sibling may not try. They give it up. For her sake, I hope she doesn't claim the Duchy. Otherwise…" She opens her first and made an explosion sound. "Well, you know."

"You guys are brutal."

"Our world is brutal." Rego kicks his feet up onto the table. "You live on a nice, warm planet with a cozy atmosphere blocking out cosmic rays. We live in an icy desert, with little oxygen and radiation blasting away at our chromosomes. Shorter lifespans. That's why we get things done. That sense of urgency—"

The glasses vibrate on the table, and drinks ripple.

"Is that Jupiter?" I ask.

"No, he's on the other side of the planet." Rego jumps up to his feet and runs out the door. Helliana, Phobos, and I follow him, nearly flipping the table over.

Droids, their metallic frames shimmering in the full moonlight, line the top of every building around us. Val and Raj stand by the entrance. Val has her arms crossed, brow furrowed, ready to destroy us all.

"Ugh, how'd they find us?" Rego pounds the computer on his arm. "This should've warned us they were coming."

"This is the part where you surrender." Val uncrosses her arms and stands up straight.

"Reinforcements?" Helliana whispers the question to Rego.

"Too far away," he replies.

"How could you betray us, Jake? How could you betray me?" Val scoops up her long red hair and twists a band around to put it in a ponytail, ready to fight.

"They betrayed us, Val. They strapped bombs to our necks. I've joined them to set all of us free. To set you free."

"Even if you win, Queen Olympia will still imprison us. We may not wear collars, but we'd be shackled some other way."

Rego unsheathes the sword and scans the tops of all the buildings. "Just look at 'em all." He eyes the dozens of droids.

"He's made his choice, and he's chosen wisely." Helliana grabs my hand.

Val shakes her head angrily. "Oh, I see. They laid out some bait for you, and you gobbled it up. I always knew you were an idiot, Jake."

"Val…"

"They questioned Emma and Aunt Gracie in prison because of you. In the same one as your mother."

"Did they let them out?" I ask.

"I'm not sure."

Phobos makes two fists. "Don't know about you all, but," magical energy surrounds his body, "I'm ready to die."

He launches himself toward a droid and plunges a foot into its face. Metal fragments fly everywhere, and then he spins around and kicks a shin through another droid's torso.

After that, magic erupts everywhere, extending from every hand from every person or droid.

Rego slashes through droid after droid, knocking away magic bullets from the droid's arms.

Helliana ducks around the first few volleys and then charges at Val, tackling her and then rolling into the front door of a building. A light sears through all the windows and doors as powerful energy rocks the tower to its foundation. Smoke pours out of the openings and the whole thing would come down in moments.

Raj shoots a beam at me that I backhand to some droids, frying them instantly. I rush at him while dodging his other follow-up blasts, the street scorching the ground where they pass.

I close the gap, throwing a power blow at Raj's face. He lifts a hand and grabs my fist in midair, but the force of it still slams his hand into his nose. A red stream trickles down from a nostril.

Droids fly in every direction. I have to trim their numbers before I can properly fight Raj. He hops backward as I follow him down. He eludes each one of my blows. I blast at droids between every jump, sometimes shattering them apart with one attack while others tear off a limb.

Raj and I separate farther from the group before he finally holds his ground, coming back at me with a series of kicks. High. Low. High. My hands sting after slapping away each leg.

One of them strikes me in the back. I careen into a wall, and my head bounces off with a thud. Two droids grab my shoulders. I kick off the wall and into the next building, the two droids on my back getting crushed.

Raj floats above the buildings, his arms spread out wide with palms facing outward. Blue flames roll around his arms. Lightning dances between his fingers. I recognize this charge-up position.

I leap down the street. Raj fires two beams that twist around each other in the air. As they got closer, they split apart, trapping me from both sides. I pick up a car and throw it at one as the other keeps tracking me. The vehicle explodes into thousands of pieces.

The other beam chases me after I turn the corner and run down a new alleyway, but out of Raj's sight, he won't know how to move it. I time an uppercut, knocking it straight up into the air, and it explodes high above the city.

Circling a few blocks, I get behind Raj as he floats between two buildings and scans his surroundings, searching for me. I levitate up behind him and plunge my knuckles into the back of his head. He crashes into the side of a building, bricks flying everywhere, before emerging out of the other side.

I land next to him with a smug grin. I haven't felt so good about beating someone. Out of the corner of my eye, magical energy flares.

Val stands above Helliana with a hand stretched down at her.

Helliana holds up her two hands in defeat. "Please. No."

"This is for Sun Li," Val says.

CHAPTER 18: DELUGE

Val's about to unload a massive blast into Helliana, who lies on the asphalt in surrender.

"Stop!" I bolt in their direction.

Val fires at me instead. I place my palms together like a prayer, jam my fingers into the front of the blast, and open my hands like a reverse clap. The beam splits in half and heads to buildings on either end of the street. The air fills with clouds of grey dust.

Continuing my charge, I cock a fist behind my head, preparing to show Val just how much stronger I'd become. She holds up her metal hand and catches the blow, but the artificial arm crumples and folds under the impact like a car's bumper in a crash. Sparks fly everywhere. Val falls to her knees and cries in agony.

I didn't mean to hit *that* hard.

"You okay?" I ask Helliana.

She stands and lurches over, unable to open one of her eyes. "Yeah."

Val squirms on the ground and moans. Those synthetic arms have nerves connecting back into the shoulder. To her, it felt like I had just crushed her entire arm.

Rego chases after two droids on the rooftops. He swings his sword in wide arcs. His laughing echoes down the empty streets. A nearby building shakes, the glass in the windows all shattering. Phobos falls out of a window with two droids wrapped around his legs. They break apart after he impacts the ground.

Raj races to Val's side. He adjusts her arm and hits a few buttons before it pops off her shoulder with a hiss of gas. She takes a few deep breaths but stops groaning as the pain receptors from the arm stop transmitting. Seeing Raj help Val like a hero or something, the ache in my chest returns, like two hearts beating against one another.

"Your turn, Raj." I slam a foot into his chest. He tumbles down the street. Most of the droids had been destroyed, so everyone else watches.

I march over, bend down, grab Raj by the collar, and punch his face. I broke his nose before Val runs over and grabs my arm.

"Stop, Jake. Stop." She kneels beside him and lifts him with one hand to fly him away. "Are you happy now?"

"Why don't you kiss him and make it all better," I say.

Her nose scrunches up in disgust at me. "Raj's gay, Jake. If you had taken five minutes to get to know someone, you would've learned that." She floats up and away. The remaining droids follow her up.

Phobos levitates after them.

"Stop. Let them go," I say.

Phobos glances over at Rego, who nods. "Yeah. Sure. Let the guy's little crush go. He's earned it, I guess." He hangs the sword over his shoulder.

Val, Raj, and the few remaining droids shrink, smaller and smaller in the sky. Pinpricks. Then gone.

Rego spins around, assessing the city. "We partied pretty hard here, and they know where we are. Let's head out and find a new spot to hold up."

We gather up Deimos and find a forest about twenty minutes away. We set up a couple of tents and even a campfire.

"Aren't we afraid of someone finding us by the smoke?" I ask.

"Who? Who's left? Besides, we could be anybody starting a fire out here." Rego skewers a piece of meat on the sword and roasts it over the fire like a caveman. "You keep beating all your old friends for me, and I'll have to make you my new right-hand man. I might have an opening." He glimpses over at Deimos, lying on the ground, a pillow braced under his head.

"I'm afraid of what you ask your right hand to do." I make a pumping gesture.

"See, a well-timed gutter humor joke. Excellent right-hand man kind of stuff."

"Deimos is not doing much better." Helliana moves the hair out of his face. A blanket wraps him up into a Martian burrito. "No fever, though."

"Let's call down a pod and get him on a ship." Rego pushes a few buttons on his armband.

A few minutes later a metal room with an engine attached to it crashes down from the sky, breaking some of the branches of nearby trees as it comes down. It looks like an escape pod for a spaceship, the kind I'd only seen in movies. They put Deimos inside, and it launches higher and higher into the sky.

"What about you, Helliana." Rego holds a finger above his armband. "Think you need to head home?"

"Maybe later. I might be okay. Besides, I thought we'd celebrate with some redcaps."

"Oh, you know all the best squishy doors into the dark crevices of my heart." Rego digs through a duffle bag and retrieves a pouch with small red discs resembling pepperoni slices. "Yes, let's celebrate. Our little invasion is nearly over, and we couldn't have done it without you, Jake. Here, you have the first taste." He places a few of the discs into my outstretched hand.

"What are they?"

"Mushrooms from our world. Magic," Rego says. "If you have enough of them, it'll transport you to Mars."

"Really?"

"No, you gullible little idiot. Just eat 'em."

I shove the handful into my mouth. They taste like burnt bacon and are so chewy that my teeth almost bounce off when trying to crush them. "Aren't you guys going to have any?"

"We're going to watch you first. That's just as fun." Rego pokes a stick at the flames. "Takes a while to kick in anyway. I wanted to talk to you about something."

"I've already had the talk. I know that babies come from storks."

"Always a jokester. I like that. Don't take life so seriously because it'll make your hair fall out." He rubs his bald head. "Let me ask you a question. Have you seen this person before?" Rego holds up his screen. The image is of Rego and a familiar man, much thinner than last I'd seen him. His skin sags at the neck. He smiles, just a little bit. His eyes always look like a hurt puppy.

"That's… that's my Dad. But how did you know him? He died years ago as a rebel." In the background of the image is a red desert. Could that be Mars?

"I got some news for you, kid. Your old man's alive."

"That can't be. Like I said, Earth forces killed him a long time ago."

"That's what they want you to think. We helped your old man escape." Rego winks.

"You knew and only just now thought to tell me?

"Thousands of people are named Jake on this freaking planet. How am I supposed to know you're related? You look a little alike, but he's had a beard since I've seen him."

I don't know what to say now. Mom has told me so many stories about Dad and made him out to be such a big hero. "Can I talk to him?"

"No. We can't broadcast there easily, and there's a nine-minute delay. Not exactly the best voice chat. You're going to meet him when we bring you back."

After all this time, he's been alive. He couldn't have gotten in touch with me, though, right? It didn't make sense. He was on a whole other planet. Couldn't he try? There wasn't anything Earth could do.

Oh yeah, didn't I eat some weird? "How long until something happens with your little mushrooms?"

"Pretty sooooooooooo—" Rego's last word stretches out forever, changing into the long song of a whale. Time is changing, and my stomach feels queasy. He agitates the fire with his stick, orange and red flames popping out from the top, little arms and legs growing, little black charcoal spots for eyes. They flicker and dance to a song of the bird that had all flown in to the branches above and synchronized their tune. This is turning into a weird vision or something crazy.

One blue flame dances alone at the top of the fire; its eyes are bigger than the rest as it spins around, and the red and orange flames climb up closer to it. It kicks them away as they climb the summit, trying to bring it down, but the blue flame never gives up, throwing an orange flame into a red one, sending them toppling down the summit into the mountain of fire below. Two orange sparks grab the blue arms, and they spin around before exploding into puffs of smoke.

"Jake, how's it going?" A beautiful voice from far away asks my right ear, but only my right ear.

"Uh, okay." My mouth forms the words without my permission.

"I think you need some more." It's Helliana. Her eyes enlarge, like something out of a Japanese anime. Her luscious lips morph into giant red apple slices.

I shake my head, no, but my neck seems to stop on the first pass. Helliana opens my mouth and shoves in more chunks of the burnt bacon. My mouth won't move, but she opens and closes my jaw with her hand. She pushes me. I fall back to the floor, back crunching in the leaves, and sink into the ground, weighed down by the sky, which might as well have been a million pounds.

Staring up at the darkening sky, I feel like I could climb right up into it, the eternal darkness. So I do, higher and higher, until I reach a floor of light. A figure made of purple energy stands on the platform. "Jake? I wasn't expecting you." Its head glows brighter with every syllable as it speaks.

"Expecting me?" I scan the area and see nothing. No walls. No stars. Strangely, this feels more real than before sitting by the fire, like the red caps weren't affecting me here.

"Yes. The Jake I'm waiting for is different. There's no happiness left in his face. You have enough still." It cocks its head to the side. "Tell me, have you killed anyone?"

"No. I don't think so." I remember the people on the ship that I had sunk. Maybe there were people left in buildings I destroyed. "Not on purpose."

"Come back to me when you're a monster. When there's no happiness left." Its head returns to an upright position. "Time for you to go back, I think. You've been here too long."

"How long?"

"About a day in your time."

How can that be possible? I float back down. Down. Down. Through the darkness, until the stars appear, then the rough bluish line of Earth's atmosphere, then the clouds, then the tops of trees, until finally, I sink back into my body, laying right where I'd left it on the forest floor.

Not a single ember remains in the campfire. Helliana lies next to me. I can't help but feel like something's different. Rego and Phobos are both gone, but that wasn't it.

There's a constant rush. Sounds a lot like the wind through the trees. Rhythmic whooshing. Back and forth.

I stand up, almost falling over like I'd forgotten how to use my legs, and follow the sound, eventually overlooking the valley below. Water filled with debris flows back and forth. A few cars and tires float on the surface. Waves? Waves crashing into trees? Was this the…

"We're destroying the walls, Jake." Helliana leans against a tree behind me, her face still swollen from the fight.

"The walls? You. You didn't. You couldn't."

She nods. "Yes, it's the last step before returning to Mars. Rego thought you wouldn't react well to the plan so—"

"So, you drugged me? You made me trip out on some mushrooms so that you could drown millions, no, billions of people?"

Helliana's stern face doesn't change. "This was our Nagasaki, Jake. Earth would never surrender unless we did this. This is how we win."

My fingers flex, but not into fists. I feel the urge to fight her. Right there in the forest. My fingers twist and gnarl with minds of their own. Instead of bashing her, I grab her wrist, bend it towards me, and call down her pod. It lands nearby, and I shove her into it.

"Jake…"

"You're lucky you are still breathing."

She lifts off into the air with her hand pressed against the glass, glaring down at me. Helliana was a trap. Or the bait. Just as Val said, I fell for it.

They'd just used me to break apart Earth's forces until they could access the undefended jugular of the world.

It dawns on me. Mom, Emma, and Aunt Gracie are trapped in prison, buildings that will be underwater if they aren't already.

CHAPTER 19: GENESIS 7

Would it help to pray? Maybe there's something wrong about hoping that other people would die first. But I can't help it. If they were going to do it at all, I hope that they took out parts of the wall that wouldn't drown my family.

The clouds rip into smaller white puffs as I tear through the sky. Below me is the apocalypse. The roofs of buildings stick out of the water with people crammed on top like ants after a big rain storm. Chairs, tires, and all kinds of debris float through what used to serve as streets.

What can I do? I'm just one person. If they didn't have to wear collars, if they could train their powers, then they could save themselves. But thousands of people are stranded, and these are just the ones I can see. There are more all over the world. Everywhere. But I must save the ones that belong to me. That's something that I can do.

The guilt's building up so much inside that all the contents of my stomach want to come out. I want to dive into the water and never come back up.

What have I done?

What have I done?

What…

But I didn't know they'd do this. And I'm not the one that attacked the wall. They tricked me. They even drugged me so that I wouldn't stop them. I may be guilty of choosing the wrong side, but I'm not guilty of all the things the side may have done. They distracted me with the most beautiful girl I've ever seen, and not only that but she liked me back. Or, that's what they wanted me to believe. Of course, she didn't like me back. She's just some consigliere meant to blindfold an idiot like me.

It doesn't matter. They're never going to forgive me. Even if Earth somehow comes out of this, they're going to kill me along with the Martians. If Mars wins, then...I mean...should I stick with their side? God, what am I thinking? I can't ally with the monsters that would do this to all these innocent people.

Ugh, it takes way too freaking long to fly across the world. Especially when the only thing you can think about is that it's now covered in water. And that it's your fault.

Long stretches of the wall seem fine, but when I get closer to home, to what used to be green, is now covered by a blue and white smear spreading across everything. The plant, the school, my home, everything's submerged. Only the tallest buildings remain, with all the windows smashed at the water line.

Water covers everything. I don't know where to go. The whole landscape is a blue nightmare. I tap into the Martian's armband to locate the prison.

The towers at the four corners of the prison stick out of the water, but that's it. My heart falls into my stomach. Maybe they're trapped with air bubbles, or the droids had let them all out.

I inhale as much as possible, stretching my lungs until they burn, and dive in, flying underwater almost the same way as through the air. I reach the roof, channel energy into my fists, and bash through. An explosion of bubbles floats around me as I swim into the prison.

The red emergency lights glow along the hallway walls, and the crimson hue makes the place an aquatic nightmare. A droid guard walks headfirst into the wall, its limbs jerking violently. Then my body reminds me: I need to breathe.

I propel into the next room, hoping to find an air bubble against the ceiling. Dead bodies float with faces lit by the red lights. My body spasms as I push through into the next room and find the ceiling shimmering like a mirage.

Air!

I jerk my arms and legs, forgetting how to do anything but flopping toward the relief. As my face breaches the air pocket, I suck in air so fast that the water rolling off my face goes down into my chest, and a fit of coughing follows, so loud it hurts my ears.

"Where the hell did you come from?"

I wipe the water from my face. Two women, eyes wide, gawk at me. There's just enough air to show our faces. I point up. "Do you know where Jenna Ryder might be? She was a prisoner here."

"Can you get us out of here?" The younger one ignores my question and swims closer to me.

"Jenna Ryder. Where is she?"

Why? Is she your mom or something?"

"Who asks something like that in this situation? What does it matter? Yes. Yes, she's my mother, now, where is she?"

The other woman shakes her head. "Some guys came by for her last month. Dressed all in black. Psych ward got her." They took her. Took her as collateral or as bait or who knows. Should I feel relieved or more worried? She could be locked away in a basement getting tortured, asking every little thing about me, any possible weakness. "What about Emma or Gracie Ryder?"

"Don't know those names, but uh, hey, so, you gonna' save us or what?"

I snap out of my reverie. "Yeah, just grab onto my shoulder or something, and we'll get out of here." They latch onto my shoulders and press a palm against the ceiling. "Deep breath. Exhale on the way up." I'd read it in a book once where you need to breathe out; otherwise, the air in the lungs would expand and burst their lungs. It feels nice to say something intelligent for once.

Energy gathers in my palm and then fires through the ceiling and room. The air quickly escapes as a torrent of water rushes in to replace it. I fly upward, a magic bubble forming around me, but it's all too fast, and one of the women slips off. I grab her by the wrist. Something pops in her arm as we go up to the surface. Bursting out of the ocean in a foam spray, we fly over to a nearby roof that sticks out of the flood.

"You broke my wrist, jerk!"

"Sorry, just trying to save your life." I drop them off. Droids began picking people up out of the water and delivering them to rooftops. Military personnel had quickly sent out new programming to droids everywhere to start a rescue program rather than fight the Martians. The reality is that I helped destroy the droids powerful enough to fight back. I had done this.

"Aren't you going to go save more people?" The younger woman I had just saved has her hands on her hips and looks angry. Reminds me of Val.

"Nope. I'm one of the only few left who can fight them. That's what I have to do. The metal heads are saving people for now."

"What are you talking about?" She glares at me like I am an alien.

"You mean, nobody's told you that the Martians have been attacking Earth for weeks?"

She blankly stares at me. "What?"

"I'll take that as a no." The world's militaries had tried to keep it all under wraps to avoid panic. Cowards, and now all the people living near the walls were unprepared. "Gotta go."

Flying back to Tallahassee, I must check on my cousin Emma and Aunt before my conscience is free and clear. Maybe, just maybe, they weren't in that prison. I can die fighting after that, it doesn't matter, but I can't concentrate on a battle with the thought of them nagging in my mind somewhere, coming up like a pop-up window during a movie.

The tops of buildings peek out of the water, but the most incredible thing about this surreal experience is: Crap. Everyone's stuff floats on the surface. It's amazing how if you took all our things and stuff them in just two dimensions, the surface of water, it's all such a waste. Plastic containers are everywhere. This is a weird thought to have after just watching Earth get flooded and finding out your mother is locked inside the center of the planet and other family members might not be alive. Perhaps overly cerebral and philosophical internal tangents are a coping mechanism for some idiots like myself.

More important than the former prized possessions, but now floating detritus, are the people that clung to them. Droids hover above the ocean, clutching one person with one arm and snatching up the next human with the other. I save some on the way. A little girl with one ponytail sits on a pool float while crying for her mommy. I leave her on a rooftop with others, all of them asking to be saved. It'd take too much time, and I hope somebody is coming up with a plan somewhere.

Crowds of people gather on the tops of buildings like swarms of ants in a flood. I find our apartment building. Emma and Aunt Gracie stand near the edge while Val hovers with her arms crossed, her blue uniform with tears and burns all over. She has replaced her metal arm that I'd destroyed earlier with a new one.

I can tell from Emma's face that someone's told her about my switching sides. "What are you doing here?" I ask Val.

"Tried to save my family. I ended up saving yours. What are you doing here, traitor?"

"Jake, how could you?" Emma's eyes water up.

Some of the other people on the roof had gathered around, drawn at the sight of two people flying.

I'm drowning in a sea of guilt. Saying sorry won't precisely cut it. I avoid eye contact and stare down at the seawater, slapping against the side of the building instead. "I thought I was starting a revolution. Something to set everyone free from getting drained in the power plants. They made me think that we would just take over, but not this. Not this."

"Thinking was your first mistake," Val says.

"Yeah…"

"Never been a strength of yours," Emma says.

"Right…"

"I'm saying you're an idiot."

"Okay, I think we got it." I land on the building and look each person in the eyes. Val. Emma. Aunt Gloria. All the other survivors on the roof. Everyone's broken. "Isn't there anything left we can do? Isn't there a defense force forming or something?"

"Probably. I have no idea. Communications are down because there's a giant robot flying around destroying satellites." Val lands on the roof now. "There's a base where the Agent has gathered some soldiers and engineers."

"Take me there."

"Jake, you know I can't."

A dozen droids land on the roof with their arms open. People cling to them, embrace them in bear hugs, and are carried off toward the horizon to wherever the new shoreline is.

"I have to. The droids aren't strong enough to fight them, and we can still save people. They haven't destroyed all the barriers. Please. Let me do this. Let me make it up to everyone."

"Fine. If you die fighting them, then that might make up for it. Maybe. Probably not. Follow me." Val blasts off to the north.

"Bye, Emma. I'll try to make it up to you." I hug her but she keeps her hands down by her sides.

"Hurry up," Val says, appearing behind me. "Do you want to die saving the world or not?"

CHAPTER 20: BASTION

A collection of tents on the side of a mountain is the last bastion of Earth. "This is it? This is the base?" Two medic droids, red crosses painted on their chests, carry a wounded soldier on a stretcher.

"That's it." Val points to a giant metal door on the side of a cliff. "Last chance for a dry world starts right here. Let's go see Luis."

"Luis? He's here?"

"Yep. He and his brothers have been working on some new tech. They'll give us an edge in one last counterattack.

Inside is a converted hangar, but instead of aircraft, there are a ton of people milling about. Strung-up blankets and curtains form divisions between rooms. Some scientists scurry by while holding droid arms and legs stacked to their chins. There aren't any fighters upright and walking. Dozens of beds are filled with bandaged kids, some not even ten years old, lining the entire makeshift hallway.

"God, they tried throwing everything at them."

"A general was talking about sending in the mighty mites. Not even seven years old, Jake. Agent Charleston had to talk him out of it."

"So, we've already lost? Why'd you even bring me here?"

"You'll see."

Around another corner, a giant screen glows with dots all over it. Agent Charleston sits in a wheelchair with his arms crossed. He spins himself around away from the screen to face us. "Judas hasn't hung himself yet? Too bad."

"Can we just skip this part?" I ask. "I made an epic mistake. I'm an idiot. I get it. Now, what can I do to help?"

"You're lucky I don't have you executed for treason."

"Executed? Who is going to fight me here? I don't even see a high-level combat droid."

"LOOK AGAIN, JACKASS!"

Z-94 clanks up behind us. It's bigger than before, with a larger chassis, a different paint job, and a giant curved blade that has replaced its right arm.

"If it isn't my favorite AI with an IQ below 80. Good to see you, Z. Looks like you've been rebuilt with upgrades..."

"SIR, PERMISSION TO EVISCERATE THE MEATBAG?" Z-94 asks Charleston while pointing at me with the point of his colossal cutlass.

"Not yet, 94. Not yet. But as always, I appreciate your enthusiasm. You brought him here, Val. What do you think?"

"I believe him. I don't think Jake would've signed up for genocide. Pie-in-the-sky freedom nonsense, yes, that's 100% Jake's philosophy. But they tricked him just like some of the others. Besides, he's the second-strongest fighter we have now.

"Second, huh? Who's the first?"

"Marcus. Speaking of, where is he? I saw his bed was empty on the way here?" Val asks.

"He's training outside. Going to go out with the next assault team." Agent Charleston hits a button on a remote, and the TV changes from a picture of Earth to a camera set up outside. Marcus darts about, slower than usual, and with his left arm in a sling.

"He's in no shape to fight." Val snatches away the remote and turns the monitor off.

"We need every able body," Charleston says. "That body may be full of painkillers, but it's able."

"I hate to be a downer," I butt in, "but I just don't see how we can win now. There are no fighters here, and most droids don't stand a chance against them. We need to surrender."

"Quiet. You don't know anything. I can't believe we get a traitor here and then talking to me like he knows everything." Agent Charleston reaches out for the remote and Val hands it back to him. "Jake, can you shut up for thirty seconds and let me talk?"

I nod.

"Good." He changes the monitor back to the picture of Earth. "Every time any Earth forces get the upper hand against the Martians, the huge damn robot shows up."

"Jupiter."

"Jake! Thirty seconds?"

"Sorry, sorry."

"EVISCERATE?"

"No, 94. You stay quiet, too. We thought they had more than one Jupiter, but it takes a ballistic orbit and can travel around the planet in no time. They call it in whenever they start to lose, and the tide is instantly changed."

"So, we need to destroy the giant droid," Val says.

"How, exactly? It's the most powerful thing on the planet. It took out Marcus, no problem."

"We clocked its power rating." Agent Charleston shows a graph with a prominent bulge in the middle. "That huge bump there is when it fired its cannon." He switches to a slightly different chart but with another bulge in the middle. "Here's your readout from when you were once drained in a plant. Same level."

"So?"

"You can beat it, Jake."

"No. Whatever that reading was, it was an accident. I've never been or felt that strong."

"Luis thinks he knows how. See him next. He'll get you suited up. If you can beat Jupiter, the rest of the world will come out of hiding and join in the fight. Now get out of here." Charleston waves his hand like he swats away at some gnats.

Val nudges her head in another direction. "Come on. This way." She leads me to the only other room with its own door. Inside, dim but bright sparks crackle from welding and other machines putting battle droids together.

Luis wears big dark goggles to protect his eyes. He smirks and doesn't even bother saying things like the rest of them, reminding me that I'm a traitor and making me feel like crap. He jumps right into showing me all the things he'd been making.

"Here. I was only able to make three of these." Luis gestures to three swords lying on a workbench. "Getting the materials together that transmit magilectricity from human tissue to metal is difficult. Most of it gets used for droids or replacement arms."

I pick up one of the swords. "I got to use one for a little while. Rego has it now."

"Rego? Sounds like a kind of ravioli or Italian food or something. Is Rego a Martian?" I nod, and Luis continues, "Next up, I made you a new wand for your left arm."

I try to contain my giddiness, but it still comes out: "Gimme, gimme, gimme."

This one fits over your hand like a giant metal glove. The fingers mimic your own. Here. Try it on." He slips the contraption over my arm. "You might feel a little pinch," Luis says in a doctor-like tone.

The wand whirrs, and it's like a thousand bees stinging my arm at once on every square inch of me. "Holy moly, dude! "

"I've never actually tested it. How much does it hurt?"

"A lot, a ton."

"Use, say, a spicy index. Mild? Moderate? Hot?"

"Why not a one to ten scale?" Val asks.

"It's a fiery nine. A spicy nueve. Does that answer your question?" I grimace, and Luis smiles.

"You'll get used to it. It digs into your skin with needles to increase the surface area for magilectric absorption."

"How I love the science of pain." It's starting to feel better.

"Let's test it out." Luis brings me into a firing range. A humanoid figure moves about randomly. "If you open your hand, it should fire a normal blast. Hit that thing."

I spread my fingers and let loose a fireball, exploding in front of the target and sending pieces flying everywhere. The scattered parts vibrate on the floor and then put themselves back together.

"That's pretty cool, too."

"It'll be better once we get the combat droids functioning similarly. But we're still some ways out from that. Okay, next..." Luis holds up his pointer and middle finger together. "This hand sign changes the magic output to telekinetic. You should be able to pick up the target and throw it."

I copy him, holding my two fingers together, point it at the target bot, and move my hand up slightly. The target floats in the air while its single tire spins uselessly underneath it. Then I fling my arm to the side, and the target crashes into the wall, falling to bits. "Seems pretty intuitive to use." The pieces vibrate and come together again.

"Of course. We're engineers, after all. If our designs aren't easy to use, the less intelligent combatants won't be able to function with the equipment."

"Did you just call me stupid, too?"

Val walks in halfway into the conversation. "Does he need to point out the obvious?"

I give her a good glare, but she grins back.

"Uh, let's move on. The other function is holding up three fingers. That converts magic into brain waves. It should overload somebody and stun them for a second."

"I can't test this on the robotic target, so…" I point three fingers at Val. She grabs her head with one hand and the wall with the other.

"Jake... I'm going to kill you."

"I thought we weren't stating the obvious? Anyway, it works. What else?"

"That's mostly it for now. It has one more feature. Self-destruct. It's so that the wand doesn't get into enemy hands if you're about to get captured. You hold up your thumb. Like you're giving someone a thumbs up."

"That seems kind of dumb. Why not like a middle finger or something?"

Luis laughs to himself. "There's this classic movie where a droid comes from the future to stop artificial intelligence from taking over. It sacrifices itself in the end, so the technology of itself can't be used. It gives a thumbs up."

"Sounds like a terrible movie."

"As the inventor, I get to make some artistic choices. I couldn't figure out how to make it fall apart, so it uses your energy to explode. You're not likely to survive it."

"Last resort, then."

"Yup, last resort."

"Should I test it out then?" I hold up my hand and fake like I will stick up my thumb. Val and Luis scream, "No!" and stretch their arms to stop me.

I laugh. "You didn't think I would do it, did you?" Val and Luis glance at each other like *yes, yes, we did.* "As much as I like these new toys," I wiggle the fingers on the glove, "these aren't going to do much against a giant robot."

"About that," Luis pulls open a drawer and retrieves a metal plate with black straps. "Remember in Orlando when you ruined Monkoro for everyone ever again?"

"Yup, how could I forget?"

"Do you remember that I was there?"

Sure." It feels like such a long time ago.

"I had the idea to weaponize a Monkoro table."

I picture myself just throwing a table hard at someone. "What does that mean exactly?"

"On this side, the plate absorbs magic from you. Just like the chairs at the Monkoro battles."

"Okay."

"And on this side," Luis flips the plate over, "is the same material as a Monkoro table. It will project your monster here. It has a little switch on the side to activate it."

I remember the giant monster I summoned on the Monkoro table months earlier—an enormous mass of teeth and tentacles. I shudder. "How would I turn it off? I'm basically going to be inside the thing."

"I haven't thought about that part yet. I assume that you either pull it off or..."

"Or what?"

"Die, I guess."

"That's comforting." I extend two fingers and move the target all around the practice area. "How do I find Jupiter anyway? It seems like I run into it randomly."

The wheels of Agent Charleston's chair squeak as he makes his presence known. "I have a plan. And I think you're going to like it."

CHAPTER 21: IT'S RAINING CANDY

We gather in front of Charleston's monitor as Earth appears on the screen. He moves his hand in the air to control the image and flips the view over to show the eastern coast of North America. "We stopped a group here with a small remaining droid army, but the entire southeast is submerged."

"Tell us something we don't know," I say.

The agent restrains himself from slapping me. "They flew over to the west coast and tried out a new strategy, destroying the backup systems first. Right now, they seem to be partying just outside Los Angeles."

"I can confirm, first hand, that the people from the red planet enjoy celebrating every success.

"Right. It's slowed them down so much that it may be the only reason they haven't won already." Charleston takes a deep breath and closes his eyes before continuing. "LA's probably their next target, and we still haven't evacuated it yet."

"So, we head over them, catch them hung over, and slash them to pieces." I slash the air with the sword a few times. "No," Charleston says.

"No?"

"Beat them, sure. Don't get them all. Force them to call in reinforcements. Specifically, Jupiter. Then destroy it so that the rest of the world can mobilize."

"You make it sound so easy."

"Coming out of this alive is not likely. Considering you deserve a death sentence anyway, I think you will sacrifice everything to make this right."

"Uh," well, what else is there to do? "Yes."

"Okay." Charleston turns off the screen. "Z-94 will go with you. Find X-53 and make her come along. She's around here somewhere. Oh, and Marcus, too."

"Marcus? He's got one arm in a sling."

"You know the saying, 'can beat you with one arm tied behind their back?" Val asks.

"Sure." I can see where this is going, but since I'm taking volleys of insults today, I don't bother to defend myself.

"It's the same thing, but his arm's tied in front."

"Very clever. Z, you ready to kill some Martians?"

"I WAS MADE TO KILL MARTIANS."

"Sounds like a yes then."

"MY MIDDLE NAME IS KILLS-MARTIANS."

"Was that a...joke?"

Charleston wheels up to Z-94 and pats it on the side. "It's been fighting so many people that like to trade quips, Z's been learning. I'd rather it concentrate on fighting styles, but it's hard to contain the AI completely."

"A MARTIAN AND I WALK INTO A BAR. THEY DIE."

Charleston scratches his bald head. "Still has a lot to learn."

We find X-53 in a medical tent outside. A long metal chain has replaced her right forearm, and sharp metal is sticking out. She extends her left hand out toward Raj, who lies in a medical bed, asleep or unconscious. Wispy distortions of light leave her hand and enter his body.

"X, what are you doing?"

"I can help regenerate soft tissue now, but I lost telekinesis. I suppose it has been useful lately." Her voice is always soft and calm, like a mother's.

Val kisses Raj on the forehead, and a violent pang of jealousy rattles in my chest. I thought I was over this.

"Jake, I forgive you." X-53 stares into my eyes with her own creepy, almost lifeless ones.

"Thanks. You're the first to say that."

"I know that you'll make it up to us."

"I will."

"I've done what I can here. I hope that Raj will make a full recovery. I don't think he'll be forgiving you as easily."

"Probably true."

X, Z, Val, and I head outside to find Marcus. He's charging up as much energy possible into his right hand, then punches a boulder. A split second later, it shatters like glass.

"Marcus. We're going to go fight now." I toss him the third sword, and he catches it in the air.

"Okay." Now's the time I appreciate Marcus' one-word nature the most.

Let's fight.

Okay.

No questions asked. No two people in the world enjoy a good battle more than he and me.

The five of us fly toward Los Angeles, magilectric bolts flash between us, and our auras combine into a giant white ball tearing through the sky.

We arrive at a gas station out in the desert. A single road stretches off into the east and west horizons. Martians lie on their backs around the whole area, passed out and hung over from a night of drinking. It's like a frat house on a Sunday morning.

Must be about 30 of them. Probably more inside enjoying the air conditioning. "Okay. We're outnumbered, but with the swords, we should be fine. Just keep moving, don't let them grab you, and keep an eye out for each other. We need one of them to call reinforcements. Got it?" Everyone nods. The Martians all sleep through my speech. It must've been one heck of a party.

I extend two fingers of my gloved hand at a nearby car, use telekinesis to lift it high, and then rip my arm down, dropping the vehicle on two sleeping Reds. Crash! Then the car alarm starts up, causing a racket that everyone bolts upright.

"TIME TO DIE, MEATBAGS!"

Things get graphic between the swords and the squishy targets. I'm going to make myself sick unless I can picture things differently. I'll think of gross stuff as 'candy' since these Martians are just a bunch of defenseless human piñatas.

They rise from their stupors with clenched fists and determined faces. That won't last very long. We dash at them, each of us breaking off into different directions. I slash upwards across one's chest, and a rainbow of candy shoots into the air. Their expressions shift from bold to drenched with fear.

Z-94 chases after one guy trying to run away. He lifts his great blade above his head and cuts right through the fleeing Martian, then darts right through the center, sending the two halves of his body flying apart.

Z emerges from the other side with candy covering his chassis. He makes a sound like some twisted electronic laughter. "I LOVE HUMAN CANDY!"

A Red tries flying away, but Val holds out her metal arm. He stops in midair. Then she yanks her fist toward her chest, and he tumbles back in her direction. She holds out her sword until he lands on the blade like a shish kabob.

Another Martian flees into the gas station, but just before he reaches the door, X-53 lashes at him with her barbed whip, which wraps around him several times. She pulls it back, which unfurls him like a spinning top with candy spraying everywhere. He crumples to the ground, screaming.

Marcus zips back and forth between foes. A flash of his blade is all that's visible before each of them falls.

I extend three fingers at the enemy after enemy and chuckle to myself as each reaches up to clutch their head from a myoelectric wave of pain.

We make short work of them. None of them can get away with Val and me tugging them back with telekinesis. Bodies lie everywhere. "Uh, guys. We were supposed to leave them alive," I say.

"Guess we got a little excited. Haven't been able to use a sword that worked against magic fighters before." Val wipes a red coat of candy from her sword off on the clothes of one of the fallen Martians. The car alarm had stopped at some point during the massacre.

Phobos, the twin that stayed on Earth, emerges from the gas station with a hand on his head, his long hair a complete mess. "What is that noise, you guys? My head is killing me. Can we keep it down out here?"

He looks up to see the five of us standing above his dead friends and big pools of candy. His mouth hangs ajar.

"Hello." X-53 whips the ground. CRACK!

Phobos scrambles back inside, the doors sliding closed behind him.

"Oh, no, you don't." I extend two fingers at the small building and then pointed slowly to the sky. My arm shakes at the resistance. The roof and walls, cracking near the foundation, lift into the sky. Phobos clutches the magazine rack. One of the pipes bursts, and water shoots into the air like

Old Faithful. I throw my arm to the side, which sends the building crashing into the ground and breaking apart.

Phobos flies away, but I stop him in the air with telekinesis. He's stronger than the others, and I can't hold him until he slips away. Then, Val uses her power and stops him completely. We work together to bring him close. The five of us surround him as he lies in the dirt.

"Don't kill me," he pleads.

Z-94 stands over him and lifts his giant blade like an executioner.

"Not yet. Remember the plan. Let's let him call some backup. Let's keep this party going," I say.

Phobos covers his head with his forearm as if that could stop the giant droid from removing his head. "O-Okay." The quivering Martians activates his communicator. "Boss, Jake's here. He's got a few with him, but they have swords and those gloves. Took us all out. No, I don't know how they got the stuff. Just send Jupiter."

He raises his arms over his head in a fetal position. "There. Now let me go."

"Hey Z, what happens when you walk into a bar with a Martian?"

"THEY DIE!"

Gross. That's the most candy I've ever seen.

We wait for Jupiter to show up. Milling about. One of the magazines on the floor is torn in half, with a muscular dude on the front, and has a title that reads, "Get Your Hot Summer Body Shredded." Dad jokes are woven into the fabric of the universe.

"Wonder what's taking so long?" Val asks. She throws rocks as far as she can. Some of them sail off into the horizon.

"Maybe it's in the middle of fighting something." Marcus kicks dirt.

"They might be setting up a trap." X-53 cleans her whip in water, spraying up where the gas station used to be.

"Well, they better. We made short work of a lot of their guys," I say. Way in the distance, some dots approach us in the sky.

"Here come some of them." Val points off in the direction that I wasn't even facing. I spin around. A bunch of them are coming from that way, too.

"That's...a lot. From everywhere," Marcus says.

Sure enough, they've surrounded us. Then, a giant fireball rips through the clouds in the sky.

Jupiter crashes into the ground near us. The earth shakes, and my teeth chatter in my skull. The ground cracks in a dozen directions from the crater that forms from the impact. The gigantic droid stands up straight with bolts of magilectricity rippling away from its body.

Hundreds of soldiers surround us, along with this machine of death. The most eloquent poem describing my emotions somehow emerges from my lips:

"Oh, balls."

CHAPTER 22: THE ALAMO SANS TEXAS

As the lightning arcs crackle around the metal frame of Jupiter, the sweet smell of ozone makes me wrinkle my nose. Rego drops down from the sky and lands on the robot's shoulder. "Jake, Jake, Jake. Look at the mess you made."

"Really? I thought I was cleaning one up."

"Gonna' take one hell of a mop."

"You're dead." I fling my sword to the side and blood speckles, we're done with the candy thing, hit Val in the face.

"Ugh, seriously?" She wipes it off with her metal hand.

Rego jumps off Jupiter's shoulder, feet land on the ground without a sound, and walks toward me. "I always liked you, buddy. Why don't you give me those swords, and I might even let your girlfriend live." He places a hand on the hilt of the sword that belonged to Sun-Li.

"Not his girlfriend." Val fails to clean off the blood at all as it merely smeared across her face. She stops trying.

"She wishes." Her eyes are burning through me after that one. I don't even have to look at her to know.

"I still can't wrap my head around why you're so upset. How can you play innocent? You," Rego takes the sword out of his belt and points it at me, "joined us. What did you think was going to happen? We'd bounce around, blow up a couple of factories, and then all the governments of Earth would just cower before us? Let all the kids out of the power plants?"

"Yeah, that's what I hoped anyway."

"You're an optimistic little brat."

"You're an old drunk."

"I'm glad we've gotten to know each other well." Rego points back at Jupiter. "Seriously. Just surrender. I've never seen anyone survive a direct hit from our not-so-secret- weapon."

"I've seen it." I gesture at Marcus, standing with his sword before him, ready to attack at any second. Always so serious, this guy.

"I don't believe that, but if you want to make up stories to make you feel like you have a chance, then so be it." Rego heads back toward Jupiter. "Who am I to say? Probably the next ruler of Earth, but why would you care about that?"

"Doesn't Mars have a Queen? Wouldn't she be the ruler if you won?"

"Details, details. I thought you were a big-picture guy."

"THIS CONVERSATION'S BORING! TIME TO DIE!" Z-94 launches itself at Rego while his back's turned. Jupiter's giant hand slaps Z, bouncing into the ground like a stone skipping across a lake's surface.

The ring of soldiers surrounding us fire a simultaneous volley of magic. I jump straight up while the others dart off in different directions. That's when hell breaks loose. And hell's hungry.

Rego disappears into the chaos, but I have Jupiter's full attention. It braces itself as the core within its torso ignites into a magical inferno.

Errant blasts fly everywhere, potshots from the dozens of soldiers who don't know what to do with themselves with so few targets to share. I launch up in the air, keeping an eye on Jupiter as it tracks me through the sky. Just one blast from that thing, and I'm toast, literally, or maybe crispy Jake

Bacon, a product not affiliated with Jake Airlines...maybe I should concentrate on fighting.

A beam flares out from its chest, ripping through the air. I loop around like I've seen fighter pilots do in movies. A group of soldiers hover in the air, looking around like they aren't sure what to do in the maelstrom before I fly in front of them.

"Smile!" I yell. That only confuses them more as the beam following me incinerates them.

"Careful, you idiot!" Rego, sword drawn, stands on Jupiter's shoulder and slaps the side of its head in frustration.

Jupiter's core dwindles, and the beam dissipates into a puff of fading red sparkles. It launches toward me at a speed that something so big has no business doing, and I barely have enough time to form an X with my arms to block its enormous fist.

The force of the blow nearly sends me into a ballistic orbit into space. Reaching cloud level, I can't believe I held onto the sword after that punch. Jupiter, with Rego still on its shoulder, like a devil's conscience in a cartoon, comes up for a follow-up attack in a thunderous approach. The cacophony lets me know that Jupiter can't fly faster than sound, through the atmosphere at least, so I'm at least a bit faster than it.

Playing dead, I lay still until just before it gets to me when I moved slightly to the side, sword stretched out, which feels like a matador holding out a cloth as the bull ran through it.

Jupiter spins around as it passes me, releasing air from compartments in its back to jettison faster to stop; the sound of compressed air hurts my ears. I'm waiting for something awesome. Like in animes when, after the hero uses the sword, the bad guy turns around, and then his whole body slides in half.

"Hey buddy, I don't know how to tell you this, but your phallic weaponry is half the size of mine now." Rego holds his sword down near his groin in a disgusting fashion that I would never do. Ever. Really.

My sword had sheared in half. "How do I beat it?"

"You die. And then, in hell, you can dream about destroying it."

Jupiter bleeps and bloops.

Rego raises an eyebrow at the giant robot. "Yes, we're done talking. You can kill him now."

The robot powers up its cannon, the compartment in its chest glowing red.

"Hope this works." I fumble for the switch on my back for the Monkoro plate, find the plastic cover, rip it off, and flick the switch.

Thousands of tiny needles pierce into my back. "Ugh, damn you, Luis." He didn't tell me *that* would happen, though I should've known. The pain's intense as it saps more energy out of me. "Damn you, surface area." Is it working? It just hurts a lot. A small tentacle slithers over my shoulder and covers my mouth to stop my screaming.

"The hell is that?" Rego leans forward and squints.

The mass of tentacles covers me completely and grows larger. Eyes sprout all over the creature. Far below, a maelstrom of magic and dust swirls around, letting me know that Val and Marcus are still alive and killing as many of them as they can. Seeing in every direction at once gives me a glimpse into what it feels like to be God, if only in one location. I can't even process all the information, but the monster seems to act independently anyway, responding to my thoughts like a polite suggestion.

So, uh, one issue that Luis hadn't planned for. Trapped in the mass of slime and suction cup-infused limbs, I can't breathe. My body jerks for lack of air. Attack you disgusting, slimey cousin of an octopus!

Tentacles sprawl out like a web. The monster pounces for Jupiter.

"Fire! Fire now!" Rego screams.

Jupiter's cannon fires, pierces through the soft tissue, and just misses my head buried within. Rego hops off the robot's shoulder as the army of oozing arms engulfs it. The tentacles squeeze the metal frame tighter and tighter, the glass casing of the canon shatters, and the beam stops.

The cannon fire had left a hole in the monster near my face. I gasp, sucking in as much air as possible. The tissue regrows and fills in the space at an alarming rate. "No, no, no, stop! I need to breathe!"

It doesn't care.

The metal strains under the pressure and groans like a sinking ship. Jupiter swats away at the suckered arms, trying to wrap around its upper body. It grabs a tentacle with a giant fist, rips it off from the rest of the monster's body, throws the arm away, and grabs another. The dismembered arm disintegrates into a cloud of sparkles. Jupiter continues tearing off arms, but it doesn't matter, more keep growing.

My breathing hole has almost filled in, and I take one last breath before it closes off entirely. How long can I hold my breath for? A minute? Two? Hurry up and rip that scrap of metal apart!

While Jupiter focuses on fighting the larger tentacles, smaller ones work their way up from its shoulder until they encase the giant metal humanoid's arms. Other suckered limbs pull Jupiter's arms down to its sides in an oozing bear hug.

The lights throughout Jupiter's body flicker off for a moment, and the ball of entangled metal and flesh plummets into the battle below. My stomach rises up like I'm dropping down on a roller coaster ride, one that an attendant won't be able to help me escape from when I reach the bottom.

Z-94, now missing its arm with a blade on it, moves out of the way just before we crash into it. We slam into the ground, a vast dust plume billowing out of the crater we form in the ground.

With only its head and a foot exposed from the entangled mass, Jupiter's lights flash again under the strain of the most epic hug of all time.

A robotic voice crackles but still manages to say: "Self-destruct sequence initiated."

CHAPTER 23: BOOM SQUARED

Self-destruct? That isn't good. We should run. My advice goes unheeded by the monster. It clings on tighter to its metallic beast. Not only that, I'm running out of breath again. Not breathing's not exactly something I trained for.

The surviving Red soldiers bolt in every direction out of eyesight. The distance they are fleeing tells me a disturbing thing: the explosion will be massive.

"Jake is trapped in that thing." Val points to the mess of limbs flailing around the hunk of soon-to-be-nuclear metal. "How do we get him out?"

"Ten!" The countdown begins in the electronic voice. It is so considerate of its designers to include such a nice feature. I assume they also didn't want it to blow up Martian soldiers.

I can't tell them anything but would tell them to run. This is my job. Beat the giant robot. Mission accomplished.

"We have to go. No telling how big the explosion will be." Ah, Marcus, a voice of reason.

"Nine!"

"WE'LL SAVE THE MEATBAG." Z-94 charges toward the beast's center, hacking away with his massive blade. The tentacles grow back faster than it can cut them down.

"Yes, you go. We'll get him." X says. It makes sense since. X and Z would live, their consciousness are loaded up into a server somewhere.

"Okay." Val nods before she and Marcus retreat.

"Eight!"

X-53 unfurls her barb-covered whip and lashes it around in long arcs, slicing off long swathes of tentacles. Some of them reach around and latch onto her foot and back, pulling her closer into the writhing cluster. "Get him out, Z!"

"Seven!"

"DON'T NAG ME. I GOT THIS." Z-94 cuts closer and closer to the center. It looks like a farmer harvesting wheat with a giant scythe. Only the grain grows back and can wrap around everything. Z cocks its arms around for a big swing, but a dozen slimy arms curl around it just before.

"Six!"

X-53 lashes out, freeing Z just before suckered arms overwhelm her and pull her into a frenzy.

"Five!"

Z-94 pulls a twisted mess off my face. I suck in a chest full of air, the stars in my vision disappear.

"Four!"

"YOU OWE ME, TWERP." I'm so busy breathing I can't thank it. I nod.

"Three!"

Z makes one last cut around me as the monster's arms engulf his lower body and pull me free by the collar.

"Two!"

I flick the Monkoro plate back off, and all the tentacles turn into a black and crimson cloud before fading away completely. X-53 is broken into pieces and falls to the ground. Z hurls me away from Jupiter like a track athlete throwing a discus.

"One!"

An aura surrounds me as I gather enough power at the last moment to speed away. It doesn't matter.

The air rushes back toward Jupiter as it crumples in over itself. I fly in a vacuum and, for the first time, hear what nothing sounds like—the sky's black with no stars. Then, a swirling sphere of blue and black bolts grows exponentially from the center of the robot, eclipsing everything in sight.

The shockwave's wind is so powerful that I lose control of my body. My arms and legs flail around like a rag doll. I tuck myself into a ball before falling to the ground, rolling like a tumbleweed in a hurricane.

I'm lying down on the edge of a giant crater stretching at least a mile across the ground. Pain sears my lower back. I reach my hand back there and feel my warm, sticky blood. The monster summoning back plate had broken, with pieces sticking into my skin. I unbuckle the straps that hold it on and gently pull it off me before standing up.

Val and Marcus find me as I put pressure on my wounds. Had I won? A massive rush of victory washes over me. Better than the alcohol. I haven't felt genuinely victorious in…ever. "I wanted to install a pool, but I might've gone overboard with the size." I gesture to the giant crater. "What do you think?" I pluck another piece of metal from my back.

"Here they come." Val points to the horizon with her metal arm. A black swarm of shadows cluster in the sky. Martians. A lot of them.

"I thought for sure we'd be done here." The good, victorious feeling departs. I thought I'd done it. Crap.

"They're gonna finish us off." Marcus holds my broken monkoro plate. "It's what I would do."

"Me too." Val draws her sword.

I reach for my blade but remember that I'd broken it in the fight against Jupiter. "Anyone have an irreplaceable weapon I can have?"

"Fresh out." Marcus draws his blade.

"I still have this." I wiggle the fingers of my gloved hand. "What's the plan? Fight to the death or run?"

"This is most of their remaining force." Val waves her sword at the wave of Martians. "We need to do what we can. Even if it means we don't make it out alive."

The three of us stand at the crater's edge as the small army of Reds arrive. They hover in front of us over the drop, with Rego slightly ahead of the rest. "Jakey, Jakey. You destroyed my toy. That's made me a little bit upset."

"Go back to your dust bowl of a planet. You're done here."

"Not a bad idea. I do miss it." Rego lifts a hand to his face in a mocking gesture of thought. "But there's one last thing left to do."

"What's that?"

"Kill you." He snaps a finger away from his face, holding it up like the number. "Or we bring you back as a prisoner. I'll leave the choice up to you. I don't really care. Might be nice to have a little Jake head mounted in our living area."

"How about just you and me? One last duel."

"Sounds like a dumb idea. You have a lot of experience with those."

"Ask your soldiers what they think. Bet they'd rather you take on a risk rather than half of them die today."

"You can do it, boss," one Red soldier says.

"Yeah, he's weak from fighting with Jupiter. You got this," another chimes in.

Rego grunts. "Fine. Seeing as you made this nice arena for us, and I'm such a sportsman. Gladiatorial combat it is."

"Great." I reach a hand out to Val. "Can I use your sword for this one?"

"No swords." Rego sheathes his blade. "No fancy little gloves either. Let's do this the old-fashioned way. Take it off."

"Afraid I don't know how. It's kind of stuck on there. With needles and such."

"Fine, but if my guys see any funny business, they're jumping in."

I nod in agreement. We move to the center of the crater. Everyone else stood at the crater's edge.

"Not too late, Jake the Snake. Just because I bring you back as a prisoner doesn't mean it would stay that way. You can be my right-hand man. Help me take the crown away from the Queen. You'd be a general on Mars. You'll be a traitor here."

"Thanks for the offer. Let's just do this."

"Too bad." Rego draws his sword. "You'll make a nice mantelpiece, though."

I should've seen that coming. Why would he obey the rules? Before I can say anything, he charges at me while floating just above the ground, holding his sword with two hands above his head.

He slashes the blade down, aiming for my neck, but I catch it with the metal claw on my left arm, a loud clang rings in my ear. "Nice try." I unleash a blast into his chest that sends him tumbling through the dirt. Rego flips onto his feet during the roll.

Before he can react, I burst toward him. My flightpath kicks up dirt into huge clouds behind me. Rego stands as if in a baseball batter's stance. "Come get some," he says between gritted teeth.

I extend three fingers of my wanded hand and aim at his head. He drops his stance, and his face goes slack-jawed. My fist connects with his cheek, sending Rego back into the wall of the crater. I pummel into his body with a flurry of fists, left-ribs, right-face, left-face, right-ribs, over and over. I conclude with a massive uppercut that sends him flying up into the sky.

Energy gathers into my fists, and the pebbles on the ground quiver. I draw up enough energy to disintegrate him, put my hands together, and then a beam flares out to destroy the unconscious Martian.

Rego spins around midair and holds his sword in front of him. The edge of his sword meets the beam. The beam splits just before his face, the force missing him entirely.

My energy depleted, I drop my hands to my sides. "Damn it."

He zips right back down, slashing at me over and over. I duck and dodge each one, just barely, moving backward with each swipe.

"It's been fun, but let's hurry this along." Rego reaches behind him and grabs something. "Look!" The little ball explodes into a flash of light so bright that it sears my eyes.

I don't have a chance now. I can't even see him. Darkness fills my vision. Before I can move, he shoves his sword through my stomach. I grab it with my claw. The metal-on-metal vibrations tingle up my arm, but I prevent him from pulling it back out again.

The taste of blood in my mouth is the first sign this fight didn't go well. A sword sticking out of my stomach is the other. Propped up on my elbows with my face down in the dirt, I can't breathe. I wheeze, trying to suck in as much air as possible. The sword is pierced into my stomach all the way to the hilt. An army of footsteps crunches into the dirt toward me from all sides. Surrounded. That's three ominous signs if I'm counting. Which I am. The remaining Red soldiers have come in close, though I can't see anything. I can hear them.

I finally get enough air to speak, "All right," I say. Then I take in another painful gulp of air. "I'm ready."

"To give up?" Rego asks. My vision returns in a blur. They're still hazy silhouettes surrounding me, just ghosts backdropped against the horizon. The rest of his soldiers gather around to watch me die. Perfect.

"Something like that," I say.

Then I left my left arm, showing off the metal glove and giving them a hand gesture they'll never forget.

"Thumbs up, bitches."

CHAPTER 24: GESTURES

I feel silly. I'm holding up a metal-encased thumb, waiting for my arm to explode. Nothing happens.

"Are you grading the fight we just had? Thumbs? I'd go with a star system. Maybe out of five? I'd give it three and a half stars. At best." Rego searches for laughter from his soldiers but only finds some pity chuckles.

Then, some high-pitched whirring whines from the glove, and the wind blows through the crater. My body feels like pins and needles all over. Starting at my toes, all my energy rolls up in waves and packs itself into my metal glove. It glows white hot.

"Shit!" Rego lifts his sword and gets halfway down to cutting my arm off when a bright light bursts from within it.

Time slows down to a speed where I can see a hummingbird's wings flap. Red soldiers jolt backward. Rego's face peels back in layers. First the skin, then the red lasagna-like muscle, then revealing the white chalky skull. The world fades to darkness.

👍

Faces covered by surgical masks hover over me. Searing pain roars over every inch of my skin. Or what's left of it. If there's any left.

"Doctor, patient's awake," a deep voice says

"Not good. Put him under," says a soft female voice.

They shove a small plastic mask over my face.

👍

I'm back in the room of infinite darkness with the man of purple energy standing on a platform made of white light.

"Back so soon?" It shakes its head. "You certainly *look* like the part of a monster now. But no, you're not ready yet. Go back."

His platform rises higher and higher above me until it's a single scintillating star far out of reach.

👍

A soft, repetitive beep guides me out of the darkness. It's a gentle sound. The exact opposite of my alarm clock before school, which did as much to encourage wakeful consciousness as it did cause madness and misery.

I try opening my eyes, but my eyelids feel like they're made of pure iron now. Eventually, light seeps into my vision as my right eye opens like old rusty windows that haven't been used for years. Bandages blanket my left eye.

I lie in a hospital bed surrounded by sterile white walls and two humming machines on either side of me. Tubes extend out from the machines and into ports all over my bandage-riddled body. I look like a mummy. Nausea dances in my stomach, and my vision shifts like a mirage, both a result of a ton of pain meds. How much pain would I feel without them?

Recalling the sword in my stomach, I reach to check, and then I realize that my left forearm is missing. I probed my belly with my right hand, but it felt closed underneath the bandaging.

How long have I been asleep?

There's a button to call for help, but it's on the left side of the bed where I no longer have an arm and can't see. Someone must think about this stuff...come on. I lean over and press it with my right hand but almost fall out of the bed.

"Hello." A voice says over the intercom. "We're not supposed to talk to you. I've notified Agent Charleston that you're awake. He's on his way."

He's the last person that I want to see. When I get visitors in the hospital, they're friends, not someone who once strapped a bomb to my neck.

There's not even a TV in the room or anything else to do here. Just my loneliness and chemically altered thoughts. Not a good combination.

After 50% of Forever plus about thirty minutes, Charleston rolls into the room escorted by two droids, but he sees my state and probably isn't too concerned for his safety. He asks the droids to leave.

"How are you feeling, Jake?"

"Like I'm here and not. A little weirded out that I don't have an arm, but I don't care about that right now."

"You're lucky to have any arms. Or a body."

"What happened? I remember a bunch of Reds gathering around me before I lit the fuse."

The agent sets his hands on his lap and wears a smirk on his face. "Dead or captured."

"All of them?"

"Yup. You swept 'em. Marcus had to do some cleanup duty, but this Martian invasion is over."

"How'd I get back?"

"Val carried you the whole way."

"Guess I owe her one."

"One what? One life? Good luck paying that back to her."

"Yeah, especially now." I left up my bandaged stump. "What's the damage?"

Charleston goes into a long explanation about the destruction around the world. What areas are okay, and what areas are submerged? I meant the damage to myself, but I didn't want to correct him once he got started. Honestly, I don't understand him. His mouth moves, and words enter my ear, but my brain throws them in the 'maybe later' pile.

"Will I ever fight again?"

"Working on approval to get you a new arm. Like Val's. As you can imagine, most folks are busy lately. There's a little something I have to get straight with you first."

"What's that?"

"It's about how you were a double agent for us. Spying on the Martians."

"Huh? That's not what happen—"

"Ah, Jake. That blast must've shaken up your head. I told you to work with them. Remember now?"

"Noooo. Ivan led me out there, and I joined them once I found out you rigged the collars to explode."

Charleston sighs. "Do you need me to wink at you? Fine. You were a double agent." He gives me two slow winks.

Oh, I get it now. "Yes. Yes, that's right. Sorry, I'm on a lot of meds right now."

"Sure, that's the reason."

"I was a double agent. A good one. Maybe too good. I remember you recruiting me for my intelligence and almost otherworldly charm."

"I'm regretting this already." The agent slumps in his chair. I finally broke his spirit. "The government's going to try you for war crimes since you've woken up. That'll be in a couple of days."

"You'd think they'd have enough to do right now than to worry about punishing me for saving the world."

"Just because a murderer rescues an orphan from a fire doesn't mean that they aren't a murderer."

"I didn't murder anyone."

"You indirectly aided in orchestrating the biggest disaster in human history."

I lift a finger, about to try and put together some defense for my actions, but I come up with nothing. "Then why are you helping me, then?"

"Because you did save us and because you're going to help us in the future. I think." Charleston rolls toward the door. "That's all for now. Get some rest."

I stare out the window. My transparent reflection's in the glass. I'm covered in bandages except for my mouth and right eye. "Charleston. What does my face look like underneath all these wraps?"

The agent stops halfway in the doorway. "You don't want to know." Then he continues through.

The lumpy hospital bed does little in the way of providing comfort. A nurse points out that I have so many bandages, wires, and tubes running around my body that I wouldn't be comfortable even if I were on a fluffy cloud. Between that and having no entertainment at all, I'm just getting a head start on my prison sentence.

That's what they will do, right? Why go through all the trouble of executing me after trying to put me back together?

Between the infinite spaces of mind-numbing boredom and sleep, every so often, a nurse brings in a guest. The first is Marcus, and while I can't remember a single conversation that I enjoyed with him, I'm glad to have anyone to talk to.

"Yo." He sits beside my bed on my left side, where I can't see him.

"Hey, good not to see you. Can you come over on my right? My other eye is in pirate captain mode right now.

"Nah, I'm good here."

"Ooookay." That'll work. It's not like he ever made facial expressions that I need to read.

After a long moment of Marcus-styled awkward silence, he finally says, "King Tut."

"What?'

"That's what you look like. A Pharaoh or something."

"Egyptian king, huh? Well, that's not how I feel." Another long silence. I try my best Marcus impression: "How *do* you feel, Jake?" I switch back to my voice. "Glad you asked, buddy. I feel like shit. They're trying to ween me off the pain medications, which, despite the crazy dreams where dudes made of purple light try and talk to me, at least made my existence somewhat bearable. Now, my only company is the most introverted being on the planet."

Silence, then he says, "Yup."

I groan. "Why did you come, Marcus?"

"Pay my respects, I guess."

"You sound like I'm about to die or something."

"I heard that might happen."

Silence again.

"Jake, you always pushed me. If you weren't always there, willing to fight me despite all odds, I'd have never kept training. You always made me feel like if I took a break, I'd be passed by. So...thanks."

"I *did* pass you by."

"No. Don't think so."

Yes, I definitely did."

"Close, but no. Luis's little monster box doesn't count."

"That settles it. I'm going to get better and beat you with my stump." I wiggle what was left of my left arm at him. I like to think he's smiling.

"Later." Marcus closes the door behind him when he leaves.

Weeks later, the day of my trial arrives. Or sentencing. Sounds like a combo deal. The nurse brings in another guest.

"You look terrible." Val's harsh voice sounds tired. She has bags under her eyes that match those of a middle-aged mother whose kids are in a 30-hour surgery.

"You should see the other guy."

"I did. There's only a skeleton left."

"Come to set me free before my trial in a huge romantic gesture?"

Just checking in, that's all."

"Straight to business. Dang."

Val pulls a chair close to my right side so I can see her. She puts a hand on my wrist and looks me in the eyes. Er, eye. It'll take a while to get used to that. "I've been where you are. I know what you're about to go through." She holds up her metal arm and wiggles her fingers.

"You've betrayed an entire planet and were put on trial for crimes against humanity?"

"Can you just be serious for one freaking second? I'm trying to actually talk to you."

"Sorry."

"I just want you to know that if you ever want to talk…" Val's face turns to anger again. I have a crappy little grin on my face that I can't control. "I hate you."

"What? No, I want to hear what you have to say." Suppressing my grin is impossible. I don't know why. It's just so weird trying to have a seriously intimate conversation with Val.

"You look pathetic in your bandages and everything, so I'm going to say this with my eyes closed." She closes her eyes and brings her metal hand on top of mine. It's ice cold and smooth, but it still makes me feel as excited as if she'd interlocked fingers with me. "It's going to get tough. You're going to be in so much pain. But I'm there for you. I've been through it before."

My smile manages to stay tame. "Thanks Val. That means a lot to me."

She opens her eyes. "You're welcome." She examines her hands, almost confused, and then pulls them away from me. "I promise to visit you in prison. Sometimes."

"Hope I get a good lawyer."

"It's Luis."

"Luis? He's an engineer. Smart, sure, but international war crime law? Sounds like a specialization to me."

"Beggars can't be choosers, and you're one step below a beggar."

Agent Charleston knocks on the door while rolling into the room. "Jake."

"Hey, Charles. I was just about to get a kiss."

"Not even close, cowboy." Val sits back with her arms crossed.

Charleston rolls back around to leave. "It's time."

CHAPTER 25: TRIAL AND ERROR

The room they have set up in the hospital has three seats on a little stage. I don't know what they need a room like this in a hospital for. I sit in a metal chair below the stage—Agent Charleston's there but off to the side. Luis sets up a projector and screen for a presentation. He's cut off his ponytail and shaved off his facial hair. He'd transformed into some grown-up, all-business sellout.

The three representatives from the United governments have their names and their home continent on a slip of paper. One European woman, another woman from Asia, and a man from South America.

Luis wears a suit, which is odd. It's strange seeing someone our age wear formal attire like that unless we're at a wedding we don't want to go to, but if anyone's going to do it, it might as well be Luis. "Ladies and gentlemen of the tribunal, I was asked to put together a proposal of augmenting Jake to make him an unstoppable weapon in lieu of a prison sentence. I was told to think beyond the scope of any budget."

"Within reason," says the councilman from Brazil.

"Of course. First, we'll need to change his heart."

"I'm not that bad of a guy...really," I say.

"No, Jake. I mean literally, to give you an artificial heart. When you are powered up, your heart rate is over 250. Your EKG shows that your heart is already under extreme duress. Under another entire campaign, we might lose you to cardiac arrest."

"I've never been arrested."

"A heart attack."

"I know...just a joke...trying to lighten the mood here. Tough crowd."

Luis turns to the tribunal again. "He also needs extensive back surgery to support his spinal cord. During this surgery, we'll install a smaller version of the Monkoro plate, which turns him into the monster that defeated the Martian's war machine."

"If it's inside me, that means no more needles, right?"

"Correct."

"Okay, this sounds good to me. Let me be on record as saying that the fewer needles, the better."

Luis smirks, but then goes right back to business. "We'll be giving him a top-of-the-line artificial arm and leg. The arm will be capable of multi-purpose magilectric conversion similar to the glove he used to defeat the Martians. I'm still deciding on the design of the leg, but I've got a few ideas.

"You might as well tell us," says the woman from Asia.

"I'm torn between having it turn into a sharp projectile or adding systems to increase the acceleration for physical blows."

"For super karate kick action," I chime in.

"Exactly."

"You're talking about me like I'm going to be an action figure toy."

"Yes, the most expensive ever. If they don't kill you for being a traitor, that is."

"Thanks, Luis…"

"Which brings up an interesting question," the councilwoman from Germany speaks up with a heavy accent, "how do we control him? If we invest these resources for defense into one person who has betrayed us, double agent or not, how can we guarantee his loyalty? He's removed collars from himself before."

"I won't be wearing a collar. That's not happening."

"Don't worry, Jake." Luis puts a hand on my shoulder. It stings rather than provides any comfort. "Members of the tribunal, Jake has philosophical differences of opinion with the collar. It's a bit of a symbol of oppression between generations. The young powering the energy for the goals of the previous generation."

"That kind of talk is even more reason why we'd need control over him." The man from Brazil rests his hands on his stomach, his tanned, leathery fingers clasp around one another, almost forming a little jail cell.

"I'm not wearing a collar. Never. Never again."

The tribunal mumbles to each other as if I'd just declared war on them.

"I have a solution," Luis declares. "An invisible collar."

"Invisible…" I instinctively reach up to touch my neck with my left hand before realizing my arm's no longer there.

"Microscopic robots. Nano in scale. Released into the bloodstream that acts like the physical collars."

"What? No. That's the same thing."

"But it's different, Jake. You aren't wearing it around your neck like some animal."

"Yeah, that's true, but it is the same effect. I'd still be their slave."

"After what you did, you're our prisoner," says the German woman.

"He was a double agent, though." Luis lifts a finger.

"No. I wasn't. That's a lie."

Agent Charleston's slashing his throat in a gesture for me to stop. He's mouthing "*No. Stop*," and shakes his head.

"I joined them willingly because Agent Charleston rigged my collar to explode. I'm tired of being manipulated. By you." I point to Agent Charleston purposefully with my stump. "By them." I point up, meaning

Martians. "By anyone. I want to, for once in my whole life, feel free. Like I'm in control. Like I have a say in what I am and what I'm capable of."

The tribunal's quiet. Finally, the European spoke, "So, we can't trust him. Sounds like a little Martian terrorist to me."

"Now, now. He has some passion. And if you can't understand how that feels, you aren't human. Certainly, you had those thoughts back in your collar-wearing days," says the Asian representative.

"Nein," says the European. "Never."

The Asian woman rolls her eyes. "I'm not saying you're going to be free. We're deciding between the death sentence and a life sentence, I think. But let's say, hypothetically speaking, you were pardoned. What would you do?"

"I'd go to Mars."

The representatives sit up, uncomfortable, thinking I meant I'd rejoin the Martians.

"And do what?"

"Kill. Them. All."

CHAPTER 26: NO BAIL, SOME HOPE

I hate Greg. He sits behind his glass protection, equipped with an evil little grin. Sometimes, he raises the sensitivity on my collar so high that it shocks me just for being alive. He'll laugh.

I've never killed anyone outside of combat. I'm not a murderer. That's a bad thing to do. But Greg makes me reevaluate my philosophies on morality. He's there now, writing little notes. He has no work to do but is good at faking it. He doesn't want Charleston to roll in and fire him any second.

The concrete floor of my gigantic prison cell is cold to the touch. It has cracks all around it from my test fighting against new droids. X-94 sits next to me. "You're a good person, Jake," it says.

"You don't have to tell me that every five minutes."

"I'm trying to maintain your psychological health."

"Yeah, thanks. I'm fine."

"YOU ARE A SAD AND BROKEN MEATBAG." Oh yeah, Z-94 is here, too. He lords above me nonstop.

The skin under my eyepatch itches. I have yet to get any fancy replacement parts that Luis promised. My replacement arm is a hunk of junk.

A screeching sound flares over the speakers. It's Greg, my prison master. "I've adjusted Z's reactions, so it's time for another test."

"I FEEL NO PITY FOR YOU, MEATBAG. PREPARE YOUR ANGUS."

"Do you mean anus?"

"I MEAN WHAT I SAY."

Z-94 proceeds to destroy me in a spar. They've got him programmed to anticipate my every move. He's become the complete anti-Jake. X-53 heals up my cuts, and we fight again, and again, and again until there's just no energy left. Then Greg makes me sit in a power plant chair, and they sap energy from me for hours.

The death sentence would've been better.

I put my clothes back on and collapse near the window. "You have a visitor," Greg says.

Strange. I've never had a visitor before. Not after months and months.

Emma looks down at me, sighs, and frowns. "Hello, Jake."

"Hey, good to see you. How's everyone? How's Aunt Gracie?" I lurch toward the glass, and she takes a few steps away.

"Fine, fine," she says. "I just wanted to check in on you."

"And?"

"You look terrible."

I can see a smudge of a reflection in the glass. Half of my hair is still missing, permanently lost from scar tissue.

"It's a new look. It'll be in style for the zombie apocalypse."

"Glad to see you've kept your sense of humor through all this."

"It's the only thing I have that they can't take from me."

"If they leave you in here long enough, then it might die on its own."

"Thanks for that little pep talk."

"Actually, that's why I'm here."

All I can do is throw my hands up and shrug at that. What the heck is she talking about?

"Charleston couldn't visit you himself, but he wanted me to show you something." She took out her phone and plugged it into the wall. The window turned into a monitor.

A video played. It was grainy, with the camera angles jerking too fast to make anything out. Then a vast landscape of a crimson desert stretching out to the horizon before touching a pale-blue sky. A single wispy cloud hovering there. The camera must've been lying on the ground—a giant hoof stomps in front of it.

"Better luck next time," a deep voice growls. Then, the hoof rises and comes down with a crunch. Electronic snow replaces the video.

"What the heck did I just watch?" I ask.

"That," Emma turns the screen back into window mode, "was the android assault on Mars."

"Doesn't seem like it went well."

"No. It was a disaster. They're trying to figure out how to let the public know without them panicking. They're still trying to rebuild up there from that first attack."

Up there. How far down underground am I?

"Ok, so what's this got to do with me?"

"I can guess, but I'm not sure. He wanted me to give you this letter." She put a small envelope into the tray where Greg usually puts my meals. I hate Greg.

Inside the envelope isn't a lengthy love letter that you might expect from Agent Charleston. It's just a strip of paper with two words written in pen.

Be ready.

NOW WHAT?

Unleashed began as a Kindle Vella series. The story continues there!

Kindle Vella is a fiction serialization website by Amazon. Check it out.

Start with Episode 27:
https://www.amazon.com/kindle-vella/episode/B0CXMMX7M1

WHAT ELSE?

Head to www.JoshuaJamesJordan.com for short stories, other Vellas, or books that I may have.

If you're familiar with tabletop roleplaying games, I've been a regular participant of a few podcasts:

Tales of Bob & The House of Bob podcasts - www.thehouseofbob.org

Tales from the Glass-Guarded World - www.tftggw.com

Printed in Great Britain
by Amazon

45579528R00118